Pitullie Publishers

Pitullie Publishers

AKNA

ISBN 978-1-7780009-2-8 (paperback)
ISBN 978-1-7780009-3-5 (ebook)

Interior design by Aaxel Author Services
Cover design and illustrations by Paul Abraham

To my wife Madeleine,
our children and grandchildren.

I live by Mount Royal, that big rocky mountain at the centre of our city, smothered in refreshing greenery in the summer and by ice and snow in the winter. I belong to the Plateau, the overgrown village on the eastern slope of the mountain where students mix with new immigrants and where I now live whilst I attend medical school. Above all, I come from Saint-Henri and Griffintown and the streets lying about the Lachine Canal on the mountain's southern slope, where I grew up.

No city is mere geography, that is to say parks, buildings, mountains, rivers and the like. A city is its people. Montreal is incredibly rich in this regard and its inhabitants know it. We Montrealers like the panoply of races, the array of languages that envelop us.

By far the majority are French-speaking Québecois, but rare is the French-Canadian who doesn't have a drop of Irish in him or a dram of Scots. There have been successive waves of immigrants, often fugitives, Jewish, Italian, German, Hungarian, Vietnamese, Syrian, Haitian. To enumerate some is to run the risk of omitting others. The key point is that there reigns in Montreal an atmosphere of tolerance and open-mindedness that is all too rare in this world.

My Montreal is a city to walk in. Being almost four hundred years old, it has a lot of handsome buildings which embellish it and lend it atmosphere. It also has many natural features of beauty, the majestic Saint Lawrence River, Mount Royal, and near my old home, the Lachine Canal. The Canal was once a vital way past the great rapids at Lachine. It is now a handsome pedestrian park that traverses the older part of the city and every day attracts its complement of cyclists and joggers, people walking their dogs, lovers, artists, drug pushers and panhandlers.

Montreal is also an island, formed at the confluence of two major rivers, the Saint Lawrence and the Ottawa. It is hemmed in by two large bodies of water, the Lake of Two Mountains and Lac Saint-Louis, and accessed by any number of bridges. This feature gives Montreal space and breathing room.

My Montreal is a city of four seasons and four universities. The differing seasons mean change, change from sub-zero cold to summer heat wave, change from when the leaves first appear, a tender green, to when they make their dramatic departure, whirling swirls of orange and scarlet. The four universities, mercifully free of ideology and creed, are in constant but friendly competition to come up with the best students, the best professors, the best research. And the tuition fees are extremely reasonable.

The street where I was brought up is Montreal in miniature. It is like a small village, residential, but close to shops and easily accessed from the Metro, our subway system. It is shaded by big trees along one side. They block out the noise of traffic from Montreal's downtown area, which is just at hand. In twenty minutes, you can walk from the end of my old street to the entrance of a forty-storey office building in the centre of the city.

Near my old street is the Atwater Market where I used to hang out when I was younger, looking for the odd job unloading trucks or simply chatting with the good-looking women in from their farms in the Chateauguay Valley with fresh vegetables and fruit to sell. I would be fascinated by the fish on offer and wonder when it would be my turn to visit the sea, to see the Atlantic Ocean on Canada's eastern shore.

Not far from my street is a second-hand bookstore where I used to browse and dream. Behind the counter was a kind old gent, Leslie, who was always happy to discuss a book with me. Leslie wore bifocals; they gave him a particularly learned appearance. I have bought a number of books in Leslie's store over the years. My favourite authors are the Russians: Tolstoi, Dostoevsky and Solzhenitsyn.

Nearby as well is the school which I first attended. We were taught in French, and well taught. It was a good school. Next to it is a very handsome church, but I have never been inside since my father was never a churchgoer. Down the street a bit further is the Residence, where my grandad stayed.

—

I have been here many times, but still can't get used to the atmosphere when I arrive at the Residence. Outside in the street, elderly smokers are sharing their exile in silence, a cigarette packet clutched in one hand and a smoking cigarette in the other. When I pass through them I involuntarily hold my breath. The entrance doors are rebellious. At first they stick. Then they suddenly open and I find myself almost falling into the lobby. It is a windowless room and a soulless one, with black and white photographs of long-dead benefactors on the walls, and floors of brown linoleum.

There is a receptionist, one whom I do not recognise from previous visits. "I am David Forbes," I say to him, dangling a red packsack full of books in my right hand. "Here to visit my grandfather." The receptionist barely looks up, and waves me on.

A narrow corridor leads to a central area which I must pass through in order to reach Grandad's room. The chairs on either side of the corridor, placed like so many onions growing in a kitchen garden, are often occupied by silent residents.

Standing in the middle of the room beyond, a man is waving his arms and shouting. "Let me go, you bastards. Help! Help!" Two women look up briefly from their jigsaw puzzle and then resume their search for a missing piece. I edge by and head for the stairs to the first floor.

Grandad's is the third door on the left. He is installed in his big armchair by the window, his back turned towards me. "Hello, David, it's you," he guesses. "Nobody else knocks but you."

Grandad is sometimes amazingly lucid and at other times away with the fairies. There are days when he barely knows that I'm here, when he can hardly sustain a conversation.

I doubt if anyone ever loved a grandparent more than I love Grandad. He is gentle and kind. He is also my exclusive link with the past and the elsewhere. He serves as a catalyst for my thoughts and my dreams. When I sit there in the peace of his room I can let my mind wander, visit other times and other countries, imagine what he must have looked like and how he would have occupied himself at my age. Much of this is my creation, the product of my imagination. I'm not sure if I even know where Grandad was born. Somewhere in north-eastern Scotland, I think.

One of my problems, one of my realities, is that I know very little about my family. What particularly bothers me is that I know nothing at all about my mother. She and I have not seen each other since I was about two or three years of age. It is not normal, not right that this should be so, but it is the way my father has wished. It is my fate.

Grandad is warming himself in the sunlight. The most attractive thing about his room is the window and the rays of warm light that can pour in on a sunny day. By way of comparison the rest of the room seems shabby. The bed looks used, the floor is in linoleum, the dresser is of a tired shade of pale green and the Catalan carpet keeps losing bits off its edges. Just why Dad picked this place for his own father is beyond me. True, it's close to where we live, but it's not as though Dad himself visits Grandad very often or encourages me to do so.

"Hi, Grandad," I say, putting down my books and throwing my wind-jacket on the bed.

On the wall beside the bed is an old photograph of Grandad standing amidst a group of men in front of a vintage bulldozer. Most of them are wearing hard hats. There is a caption: "Radar site near Nain, 1964." There is also an old photo of my Grandma. Otherwise the walls are bare. They need paint though. There are stains and scuff marks, and bits of plaster have been chipped off.

"Nice of you to come," he says. He has now turned and is smiling at me, particularly with his eyes. They are sad eyes, but beautiful. Blue-grey, under big bushy eyebrows. They once were piercing, but now are pensive and dull. He still has a shock of hair. It is silver-white.

"I've brought you some chocolate." His face lights up. I purchased a chocolate bar for him at the corner store after Biology, my last class of the day. Not much, but my finances are tight.

He takes it gratefully and starts to unwrap it. Then he changes his mind and carefully rewraps it. "I'll keep it for later," he says. That way, he doesn't have to offer me a piece.

"It's Tuesday," he states, waiting for my confirmation.

"No, Grandad. It's Wednesday."

"Yes, of course."

The room smells of the disinfectant that they use everywhere in the Residence. "Saint Charles Residence for Seniors" it is called.

Grandad is wearing a grey wool cardigan, and under it a brown and white Viyella shirt. My father must have bought them for him. They are a sort of uniform and suit him well. On his feet are a set of slippers in caribou leather with what is left of a circle of dark brown fur around the ankle. He also has a lap rug that he can use when it gets cold, but if anything the Residence is overheated and he rarely needs it.

I go to open the window and he pulls his cardigan more closely about his shoulders but doesn't protest. He has spent most of his life in the cold.

It is springtime and a large maple tree is just coming into bloom. It is a red maple, and although the flowers are individually small, together they form a generous red mass. It has always struck me as remarkable that the red maple starts its growing season red, continues it green, and finishes it red again.

How many years is it that I have been coming to see Grandad? I think that he has been in the Residence for at least ten years now. Of course, at the beginning I would come with Dad. For the last three or four years though I have been coming alone, perhaps once every two or three weeks. I never come for very long. It seems as though a short visit means more to Grandad than a long one.

Dad once told me that Grandad had an unhappy life, that he lost money on a couple of mining ventures, that he and Grandma never really got along together. I'm not convinced. Dad sometimes says things that seem right to him at the time, but which he doesn't really mean. He's not lying, I say to myself. He's just turning it into a good story. I hate to admit it, but I'd take Grandad's word over Dad's any day.

From what I know, Grandad never lacked money. It's maybe Dad who is skimping unnecessarily, putting him in a home like this. Also, I know that Grandad loved Grandma right to the end. He told me so himself. "You see that picture on the wall, David? That's your grandmother. She was a fine woman, from Newfoundland and of Irish stock. We loved each other, but fate took her from me all too soon. Yes. All too soon."

Grandad and I sit there in silence savouring the freshness of the air that's coming in through the open window, without doubt perfumed by the red maple flowers.

Just then the door of the room opens and Jane looks in.

Jane is really nice. She has worked at the Residence as a nurse ever since I have been coming to visit Grandad. Hers is about the only permanent face; the other staff seem to be in constant flux. She is very kind to Grandad, and they seem to have a special relationship. Jane comes from Atlantic Canada, from New Brunswick. That would give her a special tie to Grandad, who spent almost all of his life further north, on the Labrador coast.

"Hello, Mr Forbes," she says to him, and then turning

to me. "Hi, David. How are the studies going?"

"Hi, Jane," I say. "They're going fine, thanks."

"Is everything alright, Mr Forbes?" She does a quick tour of the room, putting things in order, clearing a spot where she can bring Grandad a tray. "Supper in thirty minutes, Mr Forbes."

He smiles gratefully at her. "You look beautiful today," he says with great gallantry.

She laughs. "Watch out or I'll ask you to take me out for dinner. Or maybe to go dancing."

"Not on Tuesdays," he answers softly. "I never go out on Tuesdays." Jane winks at me and leaves, closing the door gently behind her.

For a while we remain silent, but that doesn't seem to bother him. When I first started visiting Grandad our conversations were more rewarding and he managed to tell me a few things about his life in Labrador. It seems that he was a self-taught engineer. I think that he went to university for one year just after the war, but then didn't have the money to continue and instead took correspondence courses. He married my grandmother sometime in the 1950s and they settled in Goose Bay. However, he spent much of his time in northern Labrador, in and about Nain, and only returned to the family in Goose Bay for occasional visits. At the time, travelling up and down the Labrador coast wasn't easy.

"Go up there yourself one day, David," he used to tell me. "The Labrador coast is very beautiful and the country behind as well. You would also like the people. They are true Canadians."

I would just laugh. "I'm a city boy, born and bred. I think I'd get lost up there."

Grandad takes pains to give me moral guidance, possibly fearing that this is lacking at home. "Choose your principles carefully, David," he once said to me. "Keep them simple, then stick to them. There are a lot of complex questions that sooner or later you will have to deal with. If you are in any kind of doubt, apply those principles. They will never let you down."

"How are your studies going?" he finally asks me. He is always eager to hear about my studies and I tell him about my courses, the other students in my class, the success or failure of the university football team, and so forth. Grandad always listens hungrily, although I can never tell how much of what I say really sinks in.

"Very well," I answer. "I start exams in three weeks' time. The first one is Statistics. That should be easy." He nods knowingly. I am in second year Biology and hope to get into medical school, and have often told Grandad that, but he invariably loses track so that I have to repeat it all over again.

When I shut the window again, Grandad stirs in his chair. He has something on his mind and makes to rise. "Can I get something for you?" I ask. He is half out of his chair, but the legs aren't cooperating. He needs help nowadays to get out of his chair. It wasn't always so, but the last two or three years have not been kind to him.

His face undergoes a curious series of changes of expression. At first it is as though he has forgotten what he had in mind. Then I can read a moment of hesitation, of reflexion. Finally, one of decision.

"Yes," he says with a slight catch in his throat, slumping back into the chair. "There." He directs me to the bottom drawer of the dresser. First, there's a heavy brown sweater; he shakes his head. Then, there's a navy-blue pyjama top; again, he shakes his head. We repeat the process several times more, but still with no luck. At the very back of the drawer there is an old silk handkerchief

with a paisley pattern in red and green. It forms a bundle and there is something heavy wrapped inside. "That," he says, pointing with his finger. I hand it to him. It sits there in his lap without explanation.

He starts to forget about the little bundle, but I am curious to know what it might contain and point at it. "What is that, Grandad?" He looks down. His fingers start fumbling at it, searching for the edge of the handkerchief.

"Would you like a hand?"

He shakes his head and continues to unwrap the bundle. It seems to take him an age. Finally, out comes a small stone. He holds it carefully in his hands and stares at it intently.

It is a carved head in a parka hood. Clearly Eskimo, or as we have now learned to say, Inuit. Perhaps six centimetres high. Its colour is somewhere between jet black and a very dark brown. "That's a nice piece," I say. "Where did you get that from?"

He doesn't answer immediately, but looks down at it for a long while and with a peculiar intensity. I can sense he is leaving me and leaving the now. He is off in another world and another time. "Where the ...," he starts to say, more to himself than to me. He then makes several other efforts to say it again. It seems to be very important to him.

"Is it from Labrador?" I prompt.

His eyes turn towards the window and as he nods his head in reply a dreamy expression comes over his face. "Labrador," he confirms. He is still trying to say something, something special. "Where the seals..." he starts. He finally gets it out in a soft whisper. "Where the seals gather."

I am increasingly curious about the little carving and reach for it so as to have a closer look. His hands close over it, so I try another tack. "I have never seen it before," I say. "Have you always had it?"

There is no reply, other than a slow shake of his head. A car's horn sounds in the street below. It is getting late. Dad will be wondering where I am, and for some reason that I can never fathom he doesn't like it when I visit Grandad. When I used to tell him that I had visited Grandad he would get angry and subject me to a long and unconvincing lecture. For this reason, I now try to keep my visits secret.

Something strange is coming over Grandad. He is looking agitated. He tries to say something, but the words fail him. He cradles the Inuit carving gently in his two hands, looking first at it and then at me. Silently, he proffers it to me.

"Would you like me to take it?" I ask. He nods slowly in the affirmative. "Just to keep it for you?" He shakes his head. "You want me to keep it for myself? As a gift?" He once again nods, his steel-grey eyes looking unblinkingly into mine. I take the carved Inuit head from him. It is surprisingly heavy.

I feel an unusual sensation. One that fills me with anticipation, and which takes me forward into the future and into the unknown. I sense that this little carving is very important to Grandad, and now also to me. Just why, I cannot tell. Looking down at it, I wonder what story it has to tell, what role it must now play. Why has Grandad given it to me? What am I now to do with it?

Why isn't Grandad giving it to my father? "Should I show it to Dad?" I ask. "Do you want me to give it to him?"

He looks up sharply and shakes his head negatively. I am surprised at the intensity of his reaction. "Thank you, Grandad," I say. "This is very special. I shall take great care of it." I place it in my trouser pocket. It feels cold against my leg. "Is that the cold of Labrador?" I wonder.

Grandad reaches for my hand and holds it for the

longest of times, looking deeply into my eyes. "Thank you, David," he whispers. "Thank you." It is as though he wants to hang on to my hand forever, to never let it go. It gives me a wonderfully warm sensation, and as I leave the room, I feel a new strength within me.

I head for home. It is a walk that I always enjoy, except perhaps in the depths of winter when it always seems that our street is the last one in Montreal to have its snow cleared.

As I arrive at our door, our neighbour Elka comes out of the basement flat. She gives me one of her massive hugs. I never knew anyone who could give a hug like Elka. I sometimes am afraid that she will also give me a kiss, but so far she hasn't. I say that, but I'm actually very fond of her. She is certainly a character. She is middle-aged and speaks with a bit of a German accent. She sometimes invites me in for a cup of tea, and maybe cake or cookies. We confide in each other, she about her finances and I about my studies. This time we greet each other rapidly, as she is heading for Atwater Market and I need to get home.

Upstairs in my bedroom, I close the door. Dad doesn't seem to have arrived yet. I take out the little head and examine it. It really is fascinating. The finely chiselled face is oval and is set in a triangular frame formed by the inside and the outside of a parka hood. The face has a smooth and prominent forehead, and a nose which curves down very elegantly to a mouth which is hardly visible. The chin is also smooth and prominent, and is strangely wide, as though the face had heavy jowls. The effect is to make the face appear slightly pear-shaped. The back of the head is pierced through by a small hole which is not visible from the front. It seems to me that the hole must have served to permit the head to be fastened to someone or something.

The more I look at the head the more it seems to reach

out to me, to bind itself to me, or perhaps more aptly me to it. There is nothing in it that I can single out or find significant, yet it seems to have a remarkable story, one that I will ultimately come to learn and perhaps even add to.

2

"Cheers, Davie. Here's mud in your eye!" Dad lifts his beer can in salute. "Keep it up," he says to me in a voice that makes it sound like a football cheer. "Go for it!"

He is referring to my marks for the year, which I just received yesterday. They augur well for my being able to get into medical school in a year's time. I take a sip of my beer. It seems awfully early in the day to be drinking beer, but when we first started out, he pressed it into my hand and left me no chance to refuse. That sums up our relationship, I suppose. One way or the other, Dad controls me every bit of the way.

Dad and I are on his cabin cruiser making steady progress up Lac Saint-Louis. This is his first outing of the year. Summer is almost here! As in past years, we have a routine. It takes us to Sainte-Anne-de-Bellevue, then all the way over to Woodlands, and then back to Pointe-Claire. I find the boat itself rather crass but enjoy the outings anyway. Mainly because Dad and I let our guard down, and generally speaking, enjoy each other's company.

The boat has an atrocious name: Miss Steak. Dad is

very proud that he had the idea although in my opinion just because an idea is clever doesn't make it a good idea. It's that Dad's main business is Leo's Steak House, down on Saint-Antoine Street west of Peel. He spends most of his day there serving up steaks to his customers. The night shift he leaves to Annie, who is his business partner and possibly something more.

We are up to full throttle now, heading along the lakeshore. Dad loves to sit at the wheel like a general leading his troops. He loves to make the boat's engine roar, to make big waves. I think that he is never happier than when he is on Miss Steak.

"One day you'll be a doctor. You'll make lots of money. Perhaps one day you'll live in one of those." He points to a large grey-stone mansion that is coming into view on our right. Its lawn is dotted with white birch trees and slopes down to the shoreline where there is a boathouse and a Laser sailboat pulled up out of the water beside it. Now that's a boat I would like to try!

"We're getting close to Sainte-Anne," he says. "May as well turn here. Look how the water is getting brown. That's the Ottawa River. Brown. When we get over towards Woodlands, we'll cross into the Saint Lawrence and the water will be greener."

I tend to think of these outings on Miss Steak in the same way as when Dad takes me to the hockey game. We go to about six games a year together, father and son, and generally have a good time. When I can't make it he goes with a friend. However there are definitely times when I find hockey games an imposition. They can get pretty boring, except maybe during the playoffs, and in any case I would sooner be settled into a comfortable chair with a good book.

When Dad divorced and I started living with him, he

hired a sort of nanny to take care of me. I think she was called Dolly, but for the rest my memories are vague. I was barely three or four at the time, perhaps less. I suppose she took care of me as a mother would. Then came school and one of the teachers in particular, Laurence she was called, took a special interest in me. I owe to Lorrie my love for English literature and my ability to compensate for my hopelessness in sports by losing myself in a good novel.

Dad drains the last beer out of his can and flips the empty over his shoulder into the water. "Don't worry," he says, noticing the expression on my face. "It'll sink."

It is getting hot on Miss Steak. "Can we stop for a swim?" I ask. Dad slows her down, looking about to see that there are no other boats around, and then stops her completely. "Go ahead," he says. I remove my T-shirt and jump overboard; he goes below to get himself another can of beer. The water is cold, but wonderful, and I splash about energetically before emerging from the lake, my skin pink and tingling.

Dad is not a swimmer. He's not in good enough shape, and that's pretty evident when he is wearing a bathing suit, which he is just now. Apart from the big belly, though, he looks pretty good. He has a square ruddy face with curly dark hair and a strong chin. It is an open face in the sense that his thoughts are immediately revealed. Or at least that is how it seems. His chest is broad and is covered by a mat of dark hair. Even his back is hairy. His arms are powerful. I wouldn't want to get into a fight with him.

I rub myself down energetically with a towel. "That felt good," I say. We start up again and Woodlands gradually comes into sight.

"How come you came home so late yesterday? Aren't your courses finished now for the summer?"

That's typical of Dad. He always wants to know what I'm up to. "I went for a quick visit to see Grandad."

"You're wasting your time," Dad says. "He has lost his marbles, all of them. I bet he didn't even know who you were."

"Just," I answer. "I also stopped in at the bookstore to have a chat with Leslie."

He doesn't believe me. "I bet you were seeing that girlfriend of yours. When are you going to bring her home?"

"One of these days," I answer. "She works, you know."

"Is she good looking? Describe her."

"Sort of blonde. Slim. Medium height. Pretty face. What can I say?" I don't add that Irene is street-smart, at times very funny, and that it's good just being with her because she's someone I can really talk to.

"I want to meet her. Watch out, Davie. Don't let her hook you for good. You know. The old honeypot."

"Don't worry, Dad. She's pretty independent." That's perfectly true, although there are times when I feel that Irene would like me to make a greater commitment.

Dad is getting thirsty again. "Like a beer?" He doesn't wait for my answer, but puts the boat on idle and disappears below to fetch two more cans of Molson's.

He's thinking again about Grandad. "There was a time when your grandad was pretty smart. He did well up there in Labrador, in construction. Does he ever talk to you about his days in Labrador?"

"Not now. His memory is slipping."

"Do you visit him often, like that?"

"Like what?"

"Like you did yesterday."

"No. Just from time to time. Why?"

"Just curious." Dad looks keenly at me. "What does

he say about life in Labrador?"

I search in my mind for an appropriate answer. Over the course of the last three or four years, I have put together some of the pieces, some inkling of what Grandad's life was like and of how Dad was brought up. Dad himself has never told me very much, if anything at all.

"He worked up in Nain," I say, thinking of the picture on Grandad's wall. "He kept his family down in Goose Bay. I guess that's where you went to school. Grandma died when she was still fairly young. She came from Newfoundland. Grandad learned to speak to the Innu and the Inuit. In their own language, I mean. Things like that. But I really don't know much more than that. I wish I did. You have never told me very much yourself."

Dad looks out over the water. "Maybe someday," he says. "I didn't like Goose Bay myself. I couldn't wait to get out of there."

"Why?"

"Everything. The long winters, the people. It was impossible to make a decent living up there."

"Grandad did."

"He's different," my father says, without explaining how Grandad was different.

I think about the small Inuit carving Grandad gave me. I wonder why it wasn't displayed somewhere so he could admire it - on his dresser for example. There must have been a special reason for him to keep it hidden in the back of his drawer like that, wrapped in a silk handkerchief. Why would he hide it? "Is it a very valuable piece?" I wonder. "Or was he hiding it from someone, from Dad for example?"

What sticks in my mind is that Grandad didn't wish me to show it to Dad. I suddenly realise that Dad is looking at me closely, trying to read my thoughts, perhaps thinking that I am holding something back. "I'm not even convinced your grandad liked it up there," he continues. "If he did he would talk about it more. Does he ever show you pictures from those days, or things he might have collected and brought back with him?"

I shrug. "You know how it is, Dad. Like you say, most of the time you can't even have a real conversation with him." I sense that I am being examined, and involuntarily turn my face away.

Dad gives a snort. "He's lost the plot, has your Grandad. Lost it completely."

We have by now turned back towards Pointe-Claire and are gradually approaching the yacht club where Dad keeps his boat. We tie up. Miss Steak looks a little dated beside some of the other boats. I'm sure Dad would love to do an upgrade.

He disappears below and emerges carrying a straw basket with a woman's bathing suit and a towel in it. "Gloria's," he explains briefly. "She forgot it last time." I have never heard of Gloria before and amuse myself trying to imagine what she must look like. The slim orange panties and generous top give my imagination plenty to work with.

We leave off some things in the clubhouse and cross the parking lot to where he left his bright red Audi.

I am troubled by my relationship with Dad. He has brought me up single-handedly. I owe everything to him: my clothing, my schooling, the roof over my head, literally everything. We have had many good times together. Notwithstanding this, I sometimes have difficulty feeling grateful to him. We disagree too often, there is too much friction between us. I am wary of him. This worries me a lot. It makes me feel guilty. "Is there something wrong with me?" I occasionally ask myself.

When we get home we share a pizza, sent over to us from the Steak House, and I curl up in my usual spot on the living room sofa with a copy of *Crime and Punishment*. Most of the books in the house are mine. Dad doesn't read much. He likes to watch American television, sports, that sort of thing.

I can hear him moving about upstairs. He seems restless. Usually, he thumps his feet hard on the floor, but tonight it is different. Then I realise why. He's not in his own room. That seems funny to me, and at first I don't react. Then I have the idea that something is wrong, or at the very least, out of the ordinary. I put my book down and go quietly to the stairs.

Dad is in my room. It's not the first time, and each time it really upsets me. Making as much noise as possible, I go upstairs to reclaim my territory. He is now out in the hall pretending to do something or other, and I go into my room. I can see that he has been in there, but doesn't want to admit it. Things have changed places. A drawer is slightly open. "I think I'll turn in now, Dad," I say. "Perhaps I got a bit too much sun today. But that was a great boat ride. Thanks very much."

"Cheers, Davie. Sleep well."

I have now closed my bedroom door and can see that Dad was in there looking for something. I check under the mattress and feel something hard. The little head is still there, safe and sound.

3

"How come you don't know your own mother, David?" It's Saturday night, and I am lying under the covers beside my girlfriend Irene. Our feet are touching at the foot of her bed, sharing their warmth and sending little messages to each other. "Explain."

"Why do you want to know? It's complicated," I answer sleepily.

"Because if you don't know your own mother, you can't understand me."

"Why wouldn't I be able to understand you?" I am beginning to wake up.

Irene gives me a quick kiss on the forehead. "Because we women are all mother figures, Dearie."

"You're not my mother. You're my girlfriend." That is an understatement, and I know it. Irene is more to me than just that. It's just that I have difficulty expressing what she means to me in my thoughts and in words.

This gets Irene going. She has a theory and wants to share it with me, at one o'clock in the morning. "When a woman marries and has children, David, she has two relationships, one with her husband and one with her children. Right?"

"Right. And which relationship is the most important?"

"That with the children of course. But both the husband and the children expect their relationship to be the most important, so the mother has to juggle them around." Irene is wide awake now and there is no holding her back.

"Are you suggesting that I view you as my mother?" I am puzzled.

"Partly. All men are the same. You see us as mothers and you also want to go to bed with us. We don't mind. We're used to it!"

"Come on, Irene. Get serious."

"I am serious. Even when you make love to us you're just trying to return to the womb."

I laugh. "You've been reading something. Freud maybe."

"No. It's just common sense. We women are happy with the arrangement too. It's much more fun to be in bed with someone else than to be in bed alone."

"In any event I think you're exaggerating. For me you're Irene, not my mother."

We lie there together in silence. She likes these sudden conversations in which her opinions are based more on intuition than on reason. Recently, however, she has been bringing up the subject of my family more and more. It seems to bother her that I live alone with my father. She has never met him, but I suppose the fact that I rarely mention him hasn't escaped her attention. I sometimes wonder if she isn't beginning to give up on me as someone capable of living a normal family life. In particular, with her.

She props herself up on one elbow and gives me a poke. "I couldn't do without my mother. She shows me all sorts of things. We talk. I tell her things I wouldn't tell my father. Do you talk much with your father?"

"Not much," I admit. "I talk more with you, and I suppose with Elka."

"That's not the same thing at all." She waits. "What do you know about your mother? What's her name? Where does she live?"

This is not the first time that Irene has brought the matter up, and I am always embarrassed. "I can't say. You know that already."

I suddenly think of the little Inuit head. "A few days ago, I visited Grandad and he gave me a little Inuit carving. A head in a parka hood. It seems very special. Perhaps the carving will lead me to her."

Irene gives a little snort. "Don't wait for a miracle. Be proactive. It's unacceptable that you should know nothing about your mother. What does your father say?"

"Dad never talks about her. As far as I know they separated soon after I was born."

"Don't you find it very strange that she doesn't want to see you from time to time, even if they are separated?"

"I think that they are actually divorced."

"That changes nothing. I would want to see my own son even if I was divorced from my husband."

"Yes, but you don't know my dad. He would do everything he could to prevent my mother from seeing me. He's like that. He's possessive."

"You should change that. Force the issue."

Irene has finished saying what she wanted to say. She now wants a bit of attention. Her hand reaches behind my neck and our conversation drifts off into oblivion as I kiss her and she moves in close to me.

Afterwards I feel just great. Not a care in the world. This is Irene's special gift to me. Thoughts of my future, my studies, even my father are light years away. We lie back in the darkness and my brain is uncluttered.

When Irene and I were at High School together we were in the same class and she sat at the desk just in front of me. I used to poke her in the back and give her hair little tugs. She pretended to complain, but I know she really liked it.

We didn't go out together then, but I used to help her a bit with her maths. She sometimes invited me back to her home after classes. Her family lived not far from our school in a duplex beside the canal. You went up a flight of stairs on the outside of the building; I think they were in wrought iron. Inside it was welcoming, but very crowded. Irene had two younger sisters and a baby brother called Max.

Irene and I would lie on the floor and do homework or play Monopoly. Later on, we also would listen to music and neck a bit, though nothing serious. She was skinny and had light brown hair that she would tie up with an elastic so that it would stick out the top of her head in a waving, golden fountain. It made her look like a jack-in-the-box. She still sometimes wears her hair that way.

Her mum, a large bluff woman with strong traces of an Irish accent, was like a mother to me. Before giving me anything to eat or drink she would have me hold out my hands so that she could inspect my fingernails. If they weren't clean I was sent off to the bathroom with a nail brush. I think that she also checked my hair for lice, but without wanting me to know.

I particularly remember one time when I was invited to Irene's for Sunday lunch, an important event in the family. Her mum had made a large pot of stew with dumplings.

During our lunch her dad, originally Italian and from Naples, bustled about helping his wife with the plates, getting us water to drink, and pouring homemade wine for himself and his wife. He continually burst into song. "He thinks he's Caruso," Irene whispered to me. At one point, he was balancing two plates of stew on his right arm and waving a carafe of red wine in the other hand. His wife looked on anxiously. "Alberto!" she cautioned. He stopped humming his little tune, grinned, and said "Two pigeons, one bean". I was mystified, and it must have been apparent because Irene, looking slightly embarrassed, leaned over to me and whispered "He says that all the time. What he means is that he's killing two birds with one stone."

"But why the bean?" I asked her when her dad had disappeared back to the kitchen.

"Because in Italy they want to catch the pigeon not to kill it. At least not immediately. That comes later!"

When Irene finished school, she trained as a coiffeuse and got a job in a hair salon in Verdun. She left home and moved into a little apartment of her own near the Lachine Canal, just across from the Atwater Market. For a while, we drifted apart.

One day, however, we bumped into each other on the street and went for a coffee in a nearby cafe. It was suddenly like old times except that we were three years older. She took me back to her apartment that night and let me kiss her and explore her body. She told me what made her happy and what didn't. At first I was awkward and afraid, and in too much of a rush. "Wait," she told me. "Not yet." When finally we came together, I realised that for the first time in my life I had really been close to somebody.

Thus started our long and happy relationship. I owe

Irene a lot. Our friendship came at a critical time in my life, and I hope that we will always be good friends even if it never becomes anything more serious.

Irene has now relaxed and fallen asleep again. I lie beside her warm body enjoying the funny little sounds she makes as she breathes, and thinking back to our conversation about mothers and about my mother in particular. "Irene is absolutely right," I say to myself. "I should know who my mother is. I should look for her. In the other broken marriages that you hear about, both parents continue to see the children. Why not Mum and Dad? And what about Mum? Shouldn't she have tried to contact me, to see me over all these years? Why didn't she?"

I reflect on the possibility that my mother may have died, but then remember the numerous times that my father has avoided talking to me about her. It would be so easy for him to say that she is dead; the mere fact that he hasn't done so suggests strongly that she is alive.

It is seven-thirty in the morning and I can hear a car door open and then slam shut in the street outside. Irene bounces out of bed and heads for the shower. I rise and pull my clothes back on. In the bathroom, I quickly smooth my hair back from my forehead and rinse my mouth. Irene is scrubbing her back with a long brush. Her body is arched back and her breasts are covered with soap bubbles. I am sorely tempted to strip off my clothes and join her. Instead, I shout "Goodbye" and "Thanks", and go out into the street. Home is fifteen minutes away by foot, and it is a wonderful sunny June morning.

"She's a marvellous girl, Irene," I think as I head up Atwater. "I'm really lucky to have her."

When I reach home, my father is moving about in the kitchen and I tiptoe past and up the stairs and into my room. It is a funny way to act, but I prefer to avoid having a conversation with him. I am starting to act like a stranger in my own house even if I have been living in it for most of my life.

After a shower, I lie on my bed and think of Irene, and then of the mother whom I don't know. Instinctively I reach under my mattress and take out the little Inuit carving that Grandad gave me. I turn it over in my hand and we seem to have a conversation. "Stay with me, little fellow," I say to it. "There could be changes coming in my life. I may need a bit of help from you."

"Don't worry," it seems to answer back, "but be prepared. It's going to be a bumpy ride."

4

Some days later, Dad and I go for supper at the Steak House. It is a warm evening and we are both wearing blue jeans and white T-shirts. We go on foot; it takes us about fifteen minutes. Dad tells me with pride how his first years in the restaurant business were difficult and how he persisted, changing the concept, improving the furniture and decor, and renegotiating the lease. "After six or seven years, things shaped up and I started to make money. I paid off my debts. That's when Annie joined me. We made a deal. And here I am today, Davie: Leo's Steak House!"

This is not the first time that Dad has said this to me. "Good going, Dad," I say. "And are you satisfied?"

This rather throws him. "Well yes, maybe. No, damn it. For all I've put into it, I should have a dozen franchises. It's the politics around here. They're a disgrace. I should have moved to Toronto long ago." He cheers up however as we arrive at the door.

The facade of the Steak House is a long picture window and over the door there is a bright neon sign saying *Leo's* in red. Just inside is a small reception desk, and to one side, an ATM. The dining area is deep and narrow, and on the walls hang numerous photographs of celebrities or would-be celebrities bearing scrawled endorsements such as "To our friend Leo", "What atmosphere!", "Best steaks in town". We go to a special table at the back near the door leading to the kitchen.

His partner Annie comes briefly to our table to greet us. "Has John been around?" Dad asks. He is referring to his friend, John Pride. They sometimes spend evenings together at the Steak House or at our home playing the financial markets on their computers.

"No," replies Annie. "No sign of John this evening. At least, not so far." She turns her head to examine two possible clients lingering outside on the sidewalk and goes off to greet them. "Shall I send you a Scotch?" she asks over her shoulder.

"Make it two," says Dad, over my protests. "We're at about breakeven tonight, Davie. Ten more guests and we're in the money."

The girl who brings us our drinks is all attention, all politeness. She is good-looking too, as is the other waitress. When she gives Dad his Scotch, he gives her waist a squeeze. "You're a pretty girl, Sue, and you know it!" She smiles and retreats hastily. "Nice ass," Dad says, looking at her back as she disappears into the kitchen.

"How's it going with your girlfriend?" he asks. I am not ready to discuss Irene with him; it's none of his business. "So-so," I say. It occurs to me that with Irene I sometimes end up discussing my father, but with my father I avoid discussing Irene.

Dad doesn't want to change subjects. He likes talking about women, girlfriends and so forth. "You don't need a girlfriend," he says. "At least a steady one. Play the field. It's more fun that way, and you have no obligations."

Dad can be pretty forward with women. He seems to take a special satisfaction in holding them by the arm or the waist, making little gestures to them, finding ways to make them take notice of him and share his smiles and his laughter. Arguably he is gallant, like Grandad is gallant. But the whole thing is different. With Grandad, it stops there; it is just a game. If anything he is trying to be nice, to give pleasure.

With Dad there is an obvious effort to carry it further. At the very least, he seems to be doing it to impress everybody else around him. I also sometimes think that he is trying to dominate the other person, to confine her in a given situation, to make her play the game his way.

Dad may be his father's son, I reflect, but the difference between them couldn't be greater. Grandad is smooth, Dad is rough.

Dad is larger-than-life, a man with strong opinions, strong likes and dislikes. One cannot fail to fall under the spell of his charm.

However, not far beneath the surface there simmers a tension. He sometimes seems like a volcano threatening to explode. There is a beast within him, waiting, always waiting to get out. You can see this when he finds himself behind a hesitant driver at a traffic light that has turned orange, or when he says something wrong and gets corrected.

"Scotch whisky is the only whisky, David." Dad interrupts my thoughts as he gestures to Sue to bring him another drink. "And the Forbes family is one of Scotland's oldest. It's a great name, Forbes. You can be proud of it." I have never known him to make any effort to find out just where in Scotland our family came from or when Grandad came to Canada. He is not a student of the past. It is the present that interests him.

More customers arrive and Dad raises his glass to them. They respond and he rises and goes over to their table for a quick chat. Suddenly he has the whole table roaring with laughter. "Who are they?" I ask when he returns.

"I don't know," he answers, "but it's always good business to make your guests welcome. You know, David, there's a lot of competition out there. This city is full of steak houses and restaurants. If you want to make money you have to hustle. It's the law of the jungle, the survival of the fittest."

Our steaks arrive with a large dill pickle and some rye bread on a side plate, as does a bottle of red wine. I must say, both the steak and the wine look pretty good. Dad knows how to lead the good life. Leo's Steak House is humming now. The noise makes it hard to carry on a conversation. Dad pours us each a glass of wine, full to the brim. He is enjoying himself.

He notices two men sitting a few tables away. "The older guy's a minister," he says to me in a subdued voice. "Or used to be. The other guy is his boyfriend. You know, Davie. Catholics, Protestants, Jews. Why do you think that there are so many religions? To say nothing of the other ones, Islam and so forth. Because no single one of them is right! Each one teaches that it is the only true religion and that the others are false. It follows that if some of them are right, then they're all false. It's as simple as that."

He lifts his wine glass. "To the female sex, David, but watch out you don't marry a religious woman. You'll end up in second place behind the minister or the rabbi."

He seems particularly pleased with this observation and decides to continue. "David. Listen to what your old man has to say. Be canny. Don't be a slave to your convictions, even less to those of anybody else. Convictions count for nothing. It's the circumstance that counts."

"I think we should also have certain principles," I say rather weakly. For a moment, I think of Grandad and what he has said to me over the years.

"Yeah, maybe. But always look about you to see what is happening. Be prepared to adapt if necessary. Sit tight when things are up in the air, and make sure you know which way the wind's blowing. That way, you'll stay out of trouble."

"I don't want to stay out of trouble, Dad," I reply half-jokingly. "I want to be a doctor." He gives me a funny look.

The Steak House is gradually beginning to empty, and Annie comes to join us at our table. I barely know her and look at her with interest. She is short, probably in her late forties, has blond hair (dyed blonde, in any case), a slender waist and generous breasts. She is wearing very little makeup. Her face is at the same time harsh and attractive. Dad pours her a glass of wine. "Hello, darling! Have a seat."

"Hello, lover boy," Annie answers with a grin as she sits down. She looks over to me. "Hi, David."

She places a large kiss on Dad's cheek and I notice her hand wandering in his direction under the table. She is buttering him up and he visibly loves it. There follows a discussion of the evening's business, staffing problems, the possibility of adding pork ribs to the menu, and other such matters. I gather that business has been falling off recently. All the same, Annie reaches into a small black purse attached to her belt and gives Dad a bundle of bank notes. He examines them briefly before tucking them into his inside pocket.

Just then the waitress happens to be on her way past us, heading into the kitchen. "Hey, Sue!" Dad calls to her, reaching out a fifty-dollar bill. "That's for you." He stuffs it into the back pocket of her blue jeans, patting her on the bum as he does so. She departs rapidly with the fifty dollars in her pocket.

I find myself uncomfortable sitting there and seeming to condone Dad's behaviour. The world has moved on, a new morality has arrived, and he seems stuck in a rut somewhere in the past. I decide to take my leave, and Dad and Annie seem relieved.

5

It is early September, and Irene and I are walking along beside the Lachine Canal. We often come here as she lives on one side of the Canal and I on the other. In any event it is a great place for a walk.

At a certain point she pauses and goes to sit on a nearby bench. "I'm tired," she explains. "I also have something in my boot." She removes the boot and gives it a shake. "One bean, two pigeons," she laughs. She seems tense though, as if there is something bothering her.

I sit down beside her. "I thought it was the other way around. Isn't it 'Two pigeons, one bean'?"

"I can never remember. In any event I prefer '*Une pierre, deux coups*.' How's it going at university?"

"Really well thanks," is my simple answer. I never say too much about my life at university to Irene. I don't want her to feel sensitive because she stopped her studies whilst I continued mine. She understands all of this instinctively and with a certain sadness. She has told me several times recently that she knows that one day we will drift apart.

A man in his thirties approaches us looking for a

handout and I give him fifty cents.

Irene approves of my gesture. "That was good of you," she says. "You're pretty generous you know." I shrug my shoulders, and she continues. "We've known each other for a long while now, haven't we? I could probably tell you a lot about yourself, David."

"Oh?"

She pulls her boot back on and turns towards me. "Yep! Three things in fact."

"Go ahead."

"First, you are a kind person. Generous. Like giving that guy some money."

"Thanks, Irene. Nice of you to say that. Next?"

"You're afraid of your father."

"Ouf! That's a low blow. This is getting a bit more serious."

"It's true, though. You keep complaining about him, but you never do anything about it. Move out! I've been on my own, now, for almost two years. Find out where your mom lives. Maybe she's somewhere here in Montreal. Perhaps you could go live with her. Act, David. Don't just mope and complain."

"You're right, you're right," is all I can manage. I am embarrassed and take a deep breath.

She comes to my rescue, sort of. "Do you want to hear the third thing I have to say about you?"

This will be her parting shot. I may as well get it over with. "Go ahead."

"You are naive. You don't look around you. You're not street-smart. You aren't perceptive."

I feel a bit indignant. I have always thought of myself as an observant person. "Give me an example."

"Yep!" she says again and thrusts a hand under my eyes. "Look at that!"

There's a ring there. It's new. "What's that? Did your mom give it to you?"

"Nope! My fiancé."

I am bewildered. "Your what?"

"George. We're engaged."

"George? Who is George? What do you mean, you're engaged? What's going on?" This is all so sudden. It's out of the blue. I have no time to react properly. I am upset. "Does George really exist?"

"Of course, he does, silly. Otherwise I wouldn't be engaged to him."

"But who is he?"

"George Parker. You don't know him. I've been seeing him for a while now and he's crazy about me."

"Irene," I stammer. "You can't be serious." All sorts of emotions are boiling up in my mind. I feel jealous of this guy George, whoever he is. I feel betrayed by Irene. I am indignant. Why didn't I see this coming? Why didn't she tell me?

I then realise that I am being a bit hypocritical. After all, I am not ready to make a permanent commitment and she may be. Still, she could have let me know. "Am I a fool?" I wonder. "Now that I am about to lose her will I realise that I really love her, that I need her?" In my heart of hearts I think that perhaps I need her, yes, but do I love her? Or to put it another way, I need somebody I can love, but is that her?

This was supposed to be a nice, quiet walk along the canal. Admiring the leaves as they begin to turn. Arm in arm with my girlfriend. Perhaps finishing with a coffee near Atwater Market. Or a kiss back at her apartment. Instead, I'm jilted and we're finished! "Do you expect to get married?"

"Of course, we do. He's very nice. I'll introduce you to

him some day."

We walk on and come to the little bridge which leads across to the neighbourhood where she has her apartment. "Goodbye, David," she says, giving me a long hug and a lingering kiss. "I hope everything turns out really well for you." As she turns away, she grabs my hand and squeezes it hard. There are tears in her eyes as well as in mine, so she quickly pulls her hand away and heads over the canal.

6

Grandad is asleep in his chair by the window. The days are getting shorter now and the sun is lower in the sky. It casts a dark diagonal shadow across his body. I have always found diagonal lines to be interesting. They are suggestive of imbalance, of movement, of change. These are interesting times for me. I am beginning to sense more movement and change in my life.

Firstly, I am in my last year of pre-med. I have deliberately chosen a number of difficult courses, so that if I can succeed in getting top grades, I will be sure of getting into medical school. Secondly, I have a new friend, Gregory, with whom I play squash and discuss politics and the facts of life late into the night. Thirdly, I have met one or two girls, and sometimes Greg and I go out together on double dates.

Gregory lives with his parents in Westmount not far above Sherbrooke Street. I have visited his house a number of times, on occasion staying for supper. It is in red brick and attached on one side. The street is quiet and shaded by tall trees. I would like to live in such a house one day.

Gregory's parents also have a country house on Covey Hill, south-west of Montreal. He says that one weekend he will invite me out for a visit. His father has a small herd of Shorthorn cattle and keeps bees. They make terrific honey. Occasionally, Gregory gives me some. It occurs to me that I should bring Grandad a small jar. He would love that.

As I watch Grandad sleeping, my thoughts wander to the little stone carving that he gave me. Ever since the time I found Dad looking through my belongings, I have suspected that his search had something to do with it. For that reason, the carving is now safely hidden outside the house. It is downstairs in the basement flat with Elka. I sometimes go down there myself to study, just to get out of the house. Elka has fixed up a little room at the back for me, with a desk and some bookshelves, and I study for hours at a time down there with my earphones on, listening to Sibelius and Rachmaninoff, and surrounded by books on stats and biology.

"Why did Grandad have the head?" I ask myself, looking around his room for clues. "Who carved it? Was Grandad that close to the Inuit community up in Labrador?"

I then recall what he said when he gave it to me. Something about the seals. I had asked him where it came from and he had answered 'Where the seals gather'. I still can't see the connection. One thing is clear, though. It comes from Labrador, is an Inuit carving and I am not to show it to my father.

I look up at the wall where the photo of my grandmother hangs. It is strange to think how little I know about my grandparents. I often wonder if that is normal. Surely, in the old days when families stayed much more together you knew your grandparents, loved them and learned from them. I have no idea who the parents of my mother were, or what they were like. My paternal grandmother died before I was born. Grandad alone I know, at least a little bit. I tell myself that I should take full advantage of that. He is so special, so kind.

Grandad used to be very generous for the native people passing through Montreal, particularly for those who came from Labrador. On several occasions when I was visiting him, especially in the earlier days when he was lucid, he would give me an envelope stuffed with a few bills and a lot of small change. "Take it around to the hostel, David. Give it to the director. Tell him it's from me. Pocket money for the people staying there."

One time when I arrived with Grandad's envelope, there was an elderly Inuit woman who had just arrived from up north accompanied by her young granddaughter. The director saw me looking curiously at them and explained that the grandmother was in Montreal for medical treatment and would be returning to her home in Labrador after a week. Meanwhile she and her granddaughter were staying at the hostel.

I knew little or nothing about Labrador, but was interested, because I knew that Grandad had worked up there. In any event, I said something polite and welcoming to the woman. Her granddaughter looked at me and then turned to her grandmother and they exchanged a few words in a language that I assumed to be Inuktitut. "I told her," the young girl said. "She doesn't speak English, only our language. She thanks you." I was struck by how the girl held herself erect, as if she wanted to appear older and taller than she actually was. She spoke very seriously, and with a charming musical accent.

At the time, I was eighteen and she seemed to be a year or two younger. She was very pretty, with a ready smile and a long face of slightly dark complexion. Her hair

was black with braids, and she had very interesting eyes, slightly almond-shaped and narrowed, that were quick and full of curiosity. She wore a sealskin thong around her wrist.

Our conversation ended there, and when the two were shown up to their room by the director I left for home. However, a little bit of that girl entered me, took life, and occupied a special corner within me.

I am still waiting for Grandad to wake up. My mind idly passes from the pretty girl from Labrador to Irene. "Is it over, then? Yes, of course it is. George! What does he look like? What does she see in him?" I start to get a bit worked up when the door opens and Jane comes into the room. Grandad is still asleep. "How is he doing?" she asks.

"Fine thanks. He seems to spend more and more of his time sleeping."

"Yes. He's slipping away gently. I'm sure he knows that you're here with him though. Keep it up." She pauses. "I think I interrupted you. What were you thinking about?"

I am not even sure myself! "My mother," I answer. "In a way, I was thinking about my mother."

"Your parents have been separated a long time, haven't they?"

"Yes. Ever since I was very young, a baby in fact. I don't even know what my mother looks like. Dad has never shown me any pictures of her. Nothing."

"He's a strange man, your father." Jane makes a frown. "Why don't you ask him?"

"I know what would happen. I've been through that before. He would explode. For a week or two, life at home would be unbearable, and in the end I would be no further ahead."

"I'm sorry about that, David." Jane hesitates, and then walks over to the cupboard. "You're taller than me. Can you get down that box? I'm sure your grandad wouldn't mind."

Together we fetch down an old shoe box. Jane takes it over to the bed and opens it. I can imagine that she has done this for Grandad from time to time as well. The box contains papers, mostly invoices, bills, that sort of thing. However, there is also an envelope with a small photograph in it. She hands it to me.

"I have to go," she says. "You can put everything back as you found it when you are finished." She has a last look at Grandad and leaves the room. I open the envelope and find a faded photograph inside. Grandad is sitting in a living room with three other persons. On the back of the picture someone has written "Goose Bay, 1986".

I can recognise Dad, just. Beside him is a woman, very pretty, probably in her mid-twenties. My heart leaps up. That could be my mother! There is another man beside her. He looks a bit younger than my father. I don't know who he might be. With my cellphone I take several copies of the photo. I start to put everything back, then hesitate. I change my mind. "Grandad," I say, shaking him by the shoulder. "Are you awake?"

He stirs and his eyes open. "Hello, David. You're there, are you?"

I show him the photo, and after a tantalising delay he smiles and raises his hand. With his finger, he points at each person in turn. "Me. Leo. Your mother. Chip."

Your mother. Those were his words. My mother! I can feel the blood rushing to my face. "What was the occasion?" I ask, looking intently at the photo.

Grandad simply nods and smiles, repeating the same answer as before. "Me. Leo. Your mother. Chip."

I want to hear it all again. "Was it a special occasion? Where were you all, Grandad?"

There is a long pause. He looks puzzled and turns the photo over and over in his hands. This time I point at each of the four people in the photo, and he identifies them in turn. "Me. Leo. Valérie. Chip."

Now I am getting somewhere! I have seen an image of my mother and know that her name is Valérie. When I ask for more information, however, he loses interest and repeats what he has already said. After a while I give up and when he goes back to sleep, I start to put everything back as it was in the shoe box. Then, on an impulse, I slip the photo into my wallet and after replacing the remaining papers in the box, and the box in the cupboard, I leave the room.

On my way home, I keep taking out the small photo and examining it. My very own mother! She looks so gentle and so kind! Her name sounds again and again in my ears. I am entranced! I absolutely must share this with someone, and who else but Greg? So I call him, and we meet for a beer near the campus.

"You only have a name, and her first name at that," Greg says after a while. "It's hard to think how you can go any further without asking your father."

"And who is Chip?" I ask. "The way Grandad said his name, it sounded very much to me like he was a second son, in effect Dad's younger brother."

"That way the picture would be of your grandfather, his two sons and his daughter-in-law. All family. That seems plausible. Have you looked for the Inuit carving? Is it there somewhere in the background?"

"No. That would be too much to hope for." We both laugh.

"Chip's a funny name, don't you think?"

"Yes, it is. I guess it's a nickname. Like Chuck, or Jim." In my head, a light suddenly turns on. "My grandmother's family name was Chipman! That settles it. Chip is family. He must be my uncle."

We down our beers, very satisfied with this discovery. "You're getting warm, David," Greg says. "Things are starting to fall into place. But to find out more about your mother, you're going to have to discuss it all with your father. Good luck, and tell me how you get on."

7

I choose a Monday in late October for a serious conversation with Dad because the Steak House is closed on Mondays. It is a sunny day, and the leaves outside are glowing orange and red in the morning sun.

We are drinking coffee in the kitchen. "Dad," I start. "I would like to know more about my mother." He pushes his chair back and takes a long look at me.

"Forget about it," he says, his face tightening.

"Is she alive?" I ask.

"I said forget about it." He then relents slightly. "I've never heard to the contrary."

"Do you ever see each other, or speak to each other?"

"No."

"But why, Dad? What went wrong between you?"

"Davie. That's between her and me. It's none of your business."

"Well, I don't know," I manage to say. "She's my mother."

"Don't let's have an argument."

"Are you divorced?"

"Of course."

"And she left me with you, just like that?"

Dad starts to get angry, but at last opens up a bit. "Just like that! She wasn't fit to be a mother. She left you with me. And you and I have gotten along fine, haven't we? I have done well by you, Davie. School. Clothes. University. All that. Forget about your mother. You're better off as it is."

He reaches for the coffeepot. "I forgot to tell you. I have some tickets to the hockey game next Wednesday. Would you like to come? Boston is playing."

"That's good of you, Dad," I say, "but I have booked a squash court for eight o'clock that night. With Greg."

"OK, OK," he complains. "I just thought I'd try."

"Coming back to my mother," I say uncertainly, "I really would like to know something about her. What is her name?"

"Davie!" he exclaims. "Just let it drop. You know I don't like talking about her."

"Why not, Dad? What's the big secret? I'll tell you then. Her name is Valérie, isn't it?"

He glares at me angrily. "Who told you that? Your grandfather, I suppose."

"Yes, it was Grandad. And what is her family name?"

"Forbes. She was only too happy to take our name. I don't remember what her name was before that."

"Where did she come from, when you met her?"

He's getting red in the face. "I don't know. Look, David. I made a great mistake marrying your mother. She was good looking, fine, but she never stopped complaining. She loved spending money. New curtains. A better fridge. She was constantly after me. Let's change the subject, OK?"

"Do you have any old pictures of her?"

"No," he protests. "Davie. I'm very fond of you. Let's not spoil that."

"Would you like to see one?" I take out my cellphone. He jumps up and pushes it away. He is looking pretty upset and his left hand is clenched menacingly into a fist. As Irene would say, there is smoke coming out of his eyes. I do my best to look at him calmly. In our silence, the tension between us increases rapidly. Each of us is now glaring at the other. Rarely have I felt so angry.

"Get out of the house," he shouts, placing his left hand on the back of my chair.

"OK," I answer, standing up. "If that's what you want."

"Go!" he says, pointing to the back door. "Get your ass out of here."

As if I wasn't moving in that direction anyway, he grabs me by the shoulder and opening the door, propels me forcibly outside. On the steps I glance back and see him standing inside with both hands on the back of the chair. His chest is heaving, and it looks as though he is about to collapse.

I go for a long walk just to let my blood come off the boil. It is so frustrating! I no longer seem able to have a normal, reasonable discussion with my father. More and more it ends up in a confrontation, like just now. In addition, there is this fixation of his of not talking to me about my mother, and for that matter about our family generally. He doesn't even like it when I visit Grandad. It's as though he's wanting to cut me off completely from the past, both his and mine. Perhaps he's hiding something, something that happened back in those years when he first met my mother, something he doesn't want me to know about.

After two hours of walking, I return home, but rather than going upstairs, I ring at the door of the basement flat to see if Elka is in. She is, and saying "Come on in!", offers me a bite of lunch. I inform her of my most recent quarrel with Dad.

"Do you find it difficult living with him?" she asks. "If so you can always move in here with me. There's a bed I can put in your study room."

I thank her, and say with a grin that one day, I may have no choice. "He'll cool down sooner or later. I don't think he enjoys our fights either."

"Perhaps you should try to do more things together. Like go to the movies or go away for the weekend. Things like that."

"You may be right. I suppose I avoid him, just so we don't start arguing. Did you get along well with your parents, Elka?" It occurs to me that I know less than nothing about her past.

She gives a melancholy smile and helps herself to a second cup of tea. "Yes, I think so," she says, "but we were living in East Germany, and when I was twelve the police came around one morning and took them both away. I never saw them again."

I am shocked. "How did you come to Canada?" I ask.

"When I was seventeen, I married a man from Berlin. Together we made plans to escape to the west. On a day in early May, we made our attempt. I succeeded, but he was blown up by a land mine. I heard the explosion and looked back, but there was nothing to see. Just a big hole in the ground. So you see, David," she smiles wryly, "we have all had our ups and downs."

I rise, and going over to her, place a little kiss on her forehead. "Thanks, Elka, and I'm sorry. You know, you are the closest thing I have to a mother." She seems very pleased at that.

The afternoon wears on, and Elka thinks that it is

time for me to leave. "You should go back upstairs, David. Maybe he will have calmed down. If not, you can always come back here for the night."

I return to the house and Dad is there in the living room watching TV. He is all charm. "I'm sorry, Davie. I blew my top, I know. It's a bad habit of mine. Just impatience, I guess. Come watch the football game. It's a replay of last Saturday's match between Edmonton and Hamilton."

I go upstairs for a moment before rejoining him. When I return, he has opened two beers and a big bag of chips.

"Who's winning?" I ask.

"The Ti-Cats, thirty to ten. Fourth quarter. Where have you been?"

"Seeing Elka," I say. "I also took a walk. I needed some fresh air."

"We shouldn't fight like that, Davie. Never. We're father and son. Promise me you won't bring up the subject of your mother again. Just to think of her makes me mad. Promise me, will you?"

I don't give a direct reply. Rather, I take a stab in the dark, one that I have been planning all day. "Tell me, Dad. Do you have any brothers or sisters? Grandad's health is declining rapidly. If something happens to him, we'll have to let everybody know."

He thinks for a while. My question has caught him by surprise, and I can see the wheels turning in his head. "Just a brother," he says. "Works somewhere up north. Baffin Island, Hudson Bay, I can't really remember." There is a long silence.

"Chip?" I ask.

He looks at me. "How do you know that? How do you know his name? Yes, Chip. But I never told you about him, did I?"

"No, you didn't. But why not? Why haven't you ever mentioned him to me? What's the point of keeping all these things secret?"

"Come on, Davie. I wasn't keeping anything secret. It's just that I had no occasion to speak to you about him. I haven't seen him for years. Lost sight of him completely. He could be dead for all I know. Or care."

"Still," I say, more than a bit shocked by his attitude, "if something does happen to Grandad, we'll have to let Chip know, won't we?"

"I suppose," is the reluctant answer.

The football game ends and we finish our beers in silence. "I suppose you are getting all of this from Grandad," he says. "Don't believe everything he says. He's no saint, you know." This makes me feel angry, but I don't let it show. For me, Grandad is without fault, and I have never heard him say anything that I would doubt.

I go to my room, shut the door and lie on my bed staring at the ceiling. My heart is pounding and I can't control it. I hate these arguments with my father. I just wish they didn't happen.

"If Irene was with me," I say to myself, "she'd know what to do."

8

Three months pass, and Grandad is fast slipping away. I can see the changes more and more. At the end, he spends a lot of time asleep. I go to stay with him as often as my courses permit, and even Dad comes on one occasion. Jane is a great help to me during these last few weeks. She knows exactly what to do and how to make it easier for Grandad, whereas I am awkward and upset.

On the day in late January when Grandad dies, I am there with him and Jane looks in from time to time. I am seated on an upright chair beside the bed where he lies propped up on his pillow. I hold his hand in mine and listen for his breathing, which is increasingly difficult to hear. His eyes are closed most of the time, and even when he does open them, he does so partially and it only lasts a short time. I imagine he is simply checking to see if I am still there.

"Grandad," I find myself saying softly to the immobile figure lying beside me, "Grandad, go to your place of peace, wherever it is. Whatever it is. I shall always remember you, keep you in my mind. Forever." Can he hear me? I don't know, but I am glad to have said it.

The breathing is increasingly inaudible and the face muscles are relaxing. His hand is growing colder in mine. Time passes. Five, perhaps ten minutes. Then I hear a little snort; the hand squeezes mine ever so slightly, and he is gone.

Death is a strange event, full of contradictions. I suppose that even as observers we all experience it in different ways, so that each of us would describe it in our own words. My grandfather's death was from his presumed point of view gradual, without pain, almost without drugs or medicine. I like to think that he was aware of what was happening, and content that it should be so.

It certainly wasn't one of those deaths that one hears about, where the last days are so full of pain and suffering that the final act is a sort of deliverance. Nor was it an act of courage, of defiance, where the deceased faces the odds, and keeps his or her composure right to the end. No, Grandad's death seemed to be an act of gradual and effortless disappearance into silence.

It was not, however, a death that was imperceptible to me. Quite the contrary, it was a major break in the course of my life. The one family member of whom I was truly fond was no more. Caring for Grandad, loving him, visiting him, thinking about him: all these things had sustained me, had brought me strength and happiness in what was otherwise a difficult home life.

Jane comes into the room as I remain there holding a now lifeless hand. She smiles softly to me and sits for a while in silence on the edge of the bed, tidying up Grandad's hair. "He was a good man," she says with ill-concealed emotion.

"Yes," is all I manage to say, there, in the silence of the room.

"Do you know what I always think of, at moments like these?" she asks. "I think of all the secrets that will never be told or revealed. Your grandad's private loves and unstated criticisms, his hidden regrets and embarrassments, his hopes and disappointments, all will be hidden forever. That's what I think of."

I try to find a suitable reply. "I think of what I should have said to him or done for him. Now it's too late." We remain silent for a while.

Jane rises from the bedside. "Well, I have to be off. There is one thing I think we should do, though. I think that someone should take charge of his papers." She points to the top of the cupboard where they are kept. I release my hand from Grandad's, and together, we go over to the cupboard and fetch the shoebox.

Taking a last look around the room she disappears with the box, saying that she will keep it safe and when she has the time, put everything into a large envelope for me. I suspect that she wants to make the box disappear before Dad discovers it.

I feel alone like I have never felt before. I badly need to go outside and get some fresh air. "Goodbye, Grandad," I say softly, as I slowly put my tuque and parka on and leave the room.

Outside the sidewalks are bare, it hasn't snowed for three days. However, the sky is grey, and the air is heavy with moisture. By the time I reach the Lachine Canal large wet snowflakes are drifting down, tickling my nose. I turn east towards the centre of Montreal, resisting the urge to cross the canal and go looking for Irene.

It is as though I am in a thick fog, not knowing where to go, not confident which direction to take. I pat my pocket to make sure I haven't forgotten my wallet. It is there. Should I stop somewhere for a coffee? But I don't feel like a coffee. In fact, I don't feel like anything. I just want to keep walking.

"Why should I continue studying?" I ask myself. "Why do I want to become a doctor? Why do I wish to continue doing anything?" Thoughts like this whirl through my mind. "What's the point? Sooner or later, we all die and are forgotten. Doctors, lawyers, shopgirls, prime ministers. We all struggle through life, only to end up in the same place."

The snow is thick and wet, driven by a damp wind that is gusting from the east. My footprints stretch out behind me whilst in front, all is becoming even and white.

My thoughts go back to Grandad. I think of how much pleasure it has given me visiting him and being kind to him. "That's all over now," I say to myself. "No more visits. There's going to be a big hole in my life."

What is my future? Where do I go from here, and why? I brush the snow from my face and neck, and pull my parka zipper up as far as it will go. The wind is penetrating and I can feel the cold. I search for an answer to my questions, and finally think I have found one.

"I have a duty to Grandad," I say to myself. "For his sake, I should continue studying and become a doctor. Yes. For his sake."

This sounds convincing enough, but is there any reason why I should have such a duty to him? I think and think. Perhaps I am beginning to figure things out. "Because there is something he wanted me to be. Or to do." A light gleams in the back of my mind. "Perhaps this is why he gave me that Inuit head!"

My feelings are calmer now, and I turn around with the wind at my back. After ten minutes' walking I find myself in front of the hostel where Grandad used to send me with his spare cash. The memory comforts me.

With a rush, I remember the elderly Inuit woman and her granddaughter whom I once met there. The girl in particular had made an impression on me. "I wonder what she's up to now?" I ask myself, as I continue on my way. I think of the Inuit head and I think of her, and gradually a link forms between them in my thoughts so that when I think of one, I also think of the other.

When I reach home, my footsteps guide me not to our front door, but to Elka's flat. I am not aware of making a conscious decision. It is as though I am simply following orders; but whose, I do not know.

When I ring at the door, Elka opens with a smile, but taking one look at me, says "What's wrong, David? You look terrible. Quick, don't let the cold in. You're covered with snow!"

She sets me down in her living room and brings me the inevitable cup of tea while I inform her of Grandad's death. "That's very sad. I'm sorry for you. I know what losing someone can be like, and your grandad meant a lot to you, I could see that."

"Yes, he did." I sit there, nursing the hot cup in my hands and feeling my fingertips tingle as they thaw out. The image of Grandad on his bed comes back to me again and again.

Elka interrupts my thoughts. "Have you seen your father? Do you think he knows?"

"They said at the Residence that they would tell him." She nods and there is a long silence.

"You should also make sure his brother knows, the uncle you told me about." I explain to her that I know nothing of his whereabouts. At the same time, it occurs to me that Grandad's death could be the occasion of my finally meeting him.

"Doesn't he work up north?" she asks. "Hudson Bay

or Labrador?"

"Yes," I answer. "It seems so."

"Then he must work for the Canadian Government," says Elka. "In any event, it's more than likely. Who else employs people in places like that?" I can't help smiling at the way she says it.

"Possibly," I say, "but I just don't know."

She is not to be put off. "I have an idea, David. Let's contact the Government office in Goose Bay. Maybe they can locate him for you."

Simple as pie! Elka is like that. She has a store of common sense that seems to enable her to sail through all the difficulties of life without a hitch. "Let's try," I say doubtfully. "It can't do any harm."

Elka rapidly reaches for her computer, finds a telephone number, dials it and hands me the phone.

"Chip Forbes? One minute, please, I'll put you through." I can hardly believe my ears. This is a miracle! I hold my breath, tightly grip the receiver, and wait. It takes a while and seems an eternity. Then he's there.

"Hello. This is Chip." The voice is pleasant. It almost sounds familiar, which of course it isn't.

"Hello." I try to speak slowly. "This is David Forbes. I'm your nephew..."

9

Dorval Airport! Have I ever been here before? I don't think so. It seems big, and very busy. Cars and taxis are competing with each other for a spot where they can let people off. Men are shouting and waving at them to get a move on. I see a sign saying "ARRIVALS", and head on in.

Three long days have gone by since my first phone call to Chip. Since then we have spoken once more, and he gave me details of his flight. I like the sound of his voice, the way he speaks. He seems to be very friendly. I can't wait to see what he actually looks like, and what he turns out to be like. He has told me what he will be wearing, and I have told him the same thing.

The notice board tells me that his flight has landed. Passengers are constantly arriving in the baggage hall. I look around and around, examining all the faces. There are so many of them. Then there he is at the foot of the escalator! We see each other almost at the same time, and he waves at me with a big smile, pointing to the carousel where he has to wait for his bag.

He is dressed in a way that immediately makes me

think of Grandad: a dark blue, double-breasted overcoat, fur hat and black leather gloves. Were it Dad, he would be wearing a Montréal Canadiens hockey jacket and blue jeans. I had best avoid making comparisons though. Otherwise who knows where they will lead me.

I go up to him and we stand there face to face. He smiles warmly, and grabs my hand, squeezing the living daylights out of it. "Firmer, David, firmer. Otherwise, one day you'll get a sore hand." I try to make my hand firmer, but it is already too late.

"I'm so happy to meet you, Uncle," I say.

"Chip." He corrects me. "Just call me Chip."

We get into a taxi and he gives the name of a hotel in downtown Montreal. "Phew!" He settles back into his seat. "I'm happy to be here. That was a long trip." He extends the word "long" in order to emphasise just how long it was. "Four, no let me see, five stops. Including Montreal of course. Next time I'll check the bus schedule."

My uncle seems to be about forty-five or fifty years old. He looks slim and fit. His face is long and tanned, with salient cheeks and chin. His hair is light brown and cut rather short. His eyes are laughing, and grey like Grandad's. He looks somewhat like Dad, although I can't quite put my finger on the similarities. However, the expression on his face is far more relaxed and friendly.

He turns towards me in the cab and examines me carefully. "Now tell me about yourself, David. What life are you leading? Where are you in your studies? That sort of thing."

I tell him in a few words, and he listens carefully.

"Are your marks good?"

"Yes, they are," I say, with a touch of pride.

"So, you'll be continuing on at university?"

"Yes, I hope to study medicine."

He nods his approval. "That's good. Now tell me about your grandfather."

As we discuss Grandad, his face becomes thoughtful. I reply to his questions. How was he when he died? Was I with him? Was he in pain? "I feel terrible, David. I should have been there. You know events sometimes creep up on you, and by the time you discover that you should have done something or been somewhere, it's too late." We drive on in silence.

Chip has been staring out the window at the buildings on each side, and then turns back to me. "I spoke to your father last night. He was very surprised that I knew about Dad's death. He will be even more surprised to learn that I am already in Montreal. Let me break it to him first. I'll call him once I have settled in at the hotel."

We are approaching the city centre and he invites me to join him for lunch the next day. I am more than happy to accept, and we agree that I should come to his hotel at one o'clock. He leaves me off near home and I stand there watching his taxi as it pulls out into the traffic.

These recent times have been difficult for me: Grandad's death, Irene, my quarrels with Dad. But now that I have met Chip, I begin to feel a lot more positive. As I watch his taxi vanishing into the late afternoon gloom, I wonder what will happen next. How will Chip and Dad get along? What will Dad say to me when he learns that it was I who contacted Chip?

My lunch the next day with my uncle is nothing short of dramatic. He tells me of the life he has led. "After leaving university, I started to work for the Federal Government, first in Ottawa, but soon afterwards up in Hudson Bay and on Baffin Island. I loved it up there."

"Which university did you go to? What did you study?"

"Well, it's a long story. I was in economics, but never

finished. It wasn't for me. So after two years, I joined the Government."

"What sort of things do you do?"

He laughs. "At first, I was like a glorified social worker, trying to help out in the native communities, both Cree and Inuit, mediating between them and the civil servants sitting glued to their desks in Ottawa."

"That must have been Grandad's influence."

"Yes, in a way. After all, I did live with him up in Nain for a couple of years after your Grandma died." Chip looks at me with interest. "Were you close to your grandad, then?"

"Very. I used to visit him often. He was..." Here the words fail me, and I can feel my chest swelling.

Chip gives me an understanding smile. "He was pretty wonderful. Of the old school. We had some great times together. I could kick myself for not having spent more time with him at the end. It was very foolish of me."

I ask Chip if he ever married.

"No. Not really. For quite a while I was living with a girl from Toronto, but in the end she found living up in the north too difficult and we split up. What about you? Have you a girlfriend?"

"Not just now," I admit, "but I'm working on it. There are one or two good-looking girls in my Statistics class." I don't mention Irene; that's finished. "When did you move to Goose Bay?"

"I was transferred about a year ago. No, a bit more. Now, I'm in a more managerial position. Less field work. Less travelling. I miss meeting the people, though." He thinks for a bit and turns to me. "You must come up to visit me in Labrador one day, David. It is God's country."

"I would love to. Just say the word and I'll come."

"Finances permitting," I add to myself, as an

afterthought.

Chip mentions that he has spoken again to my father, and that their conversation was brief and businesslike. "We will be able to talk more after the funeral tomorrow. I find him difficult to read." I shrug, as if to say that Chip will have to figure my father out for himself.

"Have you always lived together, just the two of you?"

"Yes."

"Does he have many friends?"

"He has Annie, his business partner. They sometimes go away together on his boat or for short trips. He doesn't usually bring her back to the house though. Then there's a man named John Pride. He visits us sometimes. He and Dad like to make investments together, to play the market on their computers. Apart from that Dad seems to lead a pretty lonely existence. Of course, he knows a whole lot of people who eat at the Steak House, but they never come home either."

"Does he spend a lot of time at the Steak House?"

"For sure. He runs things during the day and Annie is in charge at night. Often he spends the evenings there as well, though, having a steak and drinking with his friends."

"Has he ever been ill?"

"No. He's as strong as a bull." I pause. "Some mornings he can look a bit rocky. Probably a hangover from drinking too much the night before. He's also a restless sleeper. Our rooms are next to each other and some nights I can hear him moving around."

It suddenly occurs to me that I should show Chip the family photo, and I pull it out of my wallet. He looks at it and laughs. "That must have been taken when I was up in Goose Bay for Dad's sixtieth birthday. Leo and Valérie had just married. I sure looked different then. So did Leo. That's a good photo of Valérie."

"Chip," I say. "I know next to nothing about her. Dad never says anything. He even avoids the subject. Please tell me, what is she like?"

Chip looks surprised. "What is she like? Have you never met her? Not since she and Leo parted company?"

"No."

"That's terrible. I'm very sorry, David. How strange! But why? How come you have never met her?"

I inform him of Dad's refusal to tell me anything about her, and he frowns and shakes his head a bit. "In any event, David, set your mind at rest. Your mother is a wonderful person. A fine woman."

"I'm really happy, Chip. Just to hear that."

"Of course, I haven't seen her for a long while. Almost twenty years. She is French-speaking, originally from the Quebec North Shore, very good-looking, and with a lot of poise and charm."

"Why do you think they split up?"

"They married soon after they met, but from the first it was a stormy marriage. At the beginning they lived in Goose Bay, and then they moved to Montreal."

"That was before my time."

"Yes," Chip reflects. "You would have been born two or three years after they married, in Montreal."

The hotel dining room has now become quiet and we are the last table to remain occupied. I can see that Chip thinks that it is time for us to leave. I thank him for lunch. "I would really be grateful," I add, "if you could help me locate my mother."

"I'll see what I can do," he says. "Let's stay in touch."

10

The ceremony for Grandad is short and sweet. We are gathered together in the funeral parlour, facing a casket containing his ashes. Some flowers stand to one side.

The director of the funeral home is there with an assistant. A few friends and neighbours have come. There are one or two unfamiliar faces. From the Steak House, Annie is present with two employees from the kitchen. Elka has joined us, and Jane from the Residence. My friend Gregory is there, as is Irene.

The funeral parlour director reads a sort of prayer and then Dad says a few words. "My father was a kind man," he starts, "and a good man." He seems to have difficulty finding other things to say. More sentences follow, but they don't add much to what he has already said.

Chip then follows, and succeeds somewhat better. Meantime, I am furiously trying to think of what I will say if called upon. When Chip finishes, everybody looks at me, and I can feel my face going red.

I speak in short bursts. "I loved Grandad," I say. "I admired his kindness and honesty. I visited him often, because it gave both of us a lot of pleasure. He used to tell me about the life he led, about my grandmother, about his work. I feel lucky to have known him and to have had him as my grandad. Thank you, Grandad." I stop right there, with relief I must add, and everyone seems to think that what I have said, though short, is OK.

After the ceremony, Dad, Chip and I return home and sit down in the living room. Annie is also with us, and I notice that she is wearing a lot of makeup and sits very close to Dad on the sofa.

He has poured us all a Scotch and water, and we sit there looking down at our glasses. "Well, the old man finally cashed in his chips," he declares with a sigh.

Annie gives him a squeeze of the arm. "I'm so sorry, Leo. You were always so good to him." I am startled, and then realise that she is simply saying what Dad wishes her to say. Chip has been observing the two of them, and there is an amused look on his face.

"Tell me, Leo," he asks. "Do you think that Dad was a happy man at the end?"

"Sure. They took good care of him at the Residence. It suited him fine. It was handy for us too, easy to visit him."

"I talked a bit with Jane at the funeral. She seems very nice." Chip looks at my father and waits for his reaction.

"Jane?"

"Yes, Jane. From the Residence."

"Oh, her," exclaims Dad. "Yes, she's very nice." He is annoyed at having been caught out. Just because the Residence is near at hand and easy to visit doesn't mean that he went there very often.

I follow this conversation with curiosity. It is clear that my father and uncle are very different from each other. My father is impulsive and at times erratic, whereas Chip seems suave and self-controlled. He thinks more, and more effectively. I can already see that there is a certain wariness between them.

The two now start talking about Grandad. Dad fetches a couple of big bags of potato chips and fills up our glasses a second time. The whisky is beginning to take effect. "He was a real character," says Chip. "Another generation completely."

Dad leans back. "Do you remember those terrible jokes he used to tell? The ones about the books." He starts to laugh.

"*The Yellow River*!" Chip exclaims joyously, pointing his finger at me. "Who do you think wrote *The Yellow River*, David?" I shrug.

Dad waves a hand in the air and shouts. "I.P. Standing! And tell me the name of the well-known Chinese author of *The Spot on the Wall*." Again, a forefinger is pointed vigorously at me.

It is my turn to laugh. "I haven't a clue." The two shout in unison, "Hu Flung Dung!" They roar with laughter, like two schoolboys. The whisky is clearly beginning to take effect.

"Do you remember the one about the two-holer?" Dad starts to laugh once more. "Johnny came back from the war..."

Chip takes it on from there. "The old outhouse, it only had room for one, so Johnny pulls out a hand grenade, promising to build a new outhouse, a two-holer."

Again, Dad: "The throw is perfect, right through the crescent moon cut out of the door of the old one-holer. Bang! The grenade explodes, to the joy and amazement of everyone standing there."

Chip is whooping with laughter; the tears are pouring down his cheeks. "The smoke clears and there is the grandpère, still sitting on the pot. 'Excuse me,' he says, 'It must have been something I ate.' Or words to that effect."

"It varied," Dad adds. "Sometimes Dad changed the punchline. He would have Grandpère say, 'I'm glad I didn't let that one go in the kitchen.' Mum preferred that one." They laugh some more, and only gradually recover their composure.

"Each time he arrived from Nain, there was a celebration," Chip recalls. "He would sing some dreadful song at the top of his lungs, grab Mum by the waist, and waltz her around the kitchen."

"Yes," Dad adds, "and Mum loved it. She would look at us and pull faces."

Chip takes a sip from his glass. Dad's is already half empty. "What do we do now?" Chip asks. "I would like to take Dad's ashes back with me to Labrador. Is that fine with you, Leo?"

"For sure. Good idea. Scatter them out at sea, or in one of the rivers. Something like that."

"No. I was thinking maybe of taking them up to Nain, to bury them somewhere near where he used to live." I nod my approval vigorously.

Dad shrugs. "Sounds fine to me. Go ahead."

"You want to come?" Chip asks.

"No," Dad says. "I'm too busy."

Chip shifts in his chair. "Did he leave a will?"

"Yes. It's at the lawyer's office. I have an appointment to meet with him next week, on the morning of the twenty-eighth."

"I'll note that. I have to return to Goose Bay tomorrow morning, but I'll see if I can make it back for the twenty-eighth." I try not to show my disappointment at Chip's leaving so soon. I was hoping we could spend more time together.

"Suit yourself, but you don't need to be there. It's just

a formality."

The conversation lags. Annie is yawning and decides to go, leaving the three of us to stay on alone. Dad pours out more Scotch, and I help by passing around the potato chips.

"Do you really like it up there in Goose Bay?" Dad asks. "What's there to do? What's your job like?"

Chip explains what he does, and the talk shifts to the Innu communities of Labrador. "What a bunch of freeloaders!" Dad exclaims. "They cost us a fortune, and what do they do? Spend their whole time drinking antifreeze and sniffing glue."

Chip winces. "It's true that they have their problems, but it was very careless the way we broke their normal life cycle fifty years ago. We played a clear role in their undoing. We have an equally clear duty to help them recover."

Dad shows signs of irritation. "What life cycle? What undoing? It's inevitable. They just aren't capable of adapting to the modern world."

"Let's put this in perspective," says Chip. "There are only about three thousand Innu on the entire Labrador coast. It isn't beyond the capacity of a country of thirty-eight million to act decently and help them out."

"Maybe, but there are a lot more Indians in the rest of the country." The conversation goes on and on in a desultory manner. It is a dialogue of the deaf. Dad pours himself another Scotch. They switch now to climate change where Dad's views also jar. He thinks the whole thing is an exaggeration of the media, a plot. For a while the atmosphere becomes stormy.

Fortunately, they then begin to reminisce about the sixties and seventies, when they were being brought up by Grandma in Goose Bay. "She was a brave woman," Chip says. "Brought us up almost single-handedly. We didn't see much of Dad; he was always up north at work."

"Yes," says Dad. "I guess you're right. After she died," he recalls, "I came to look for work in Montreal. Those were tough times. I was broke most of the time."

Chip thinks back to his own past. "I joined Dad up north and worked on his construction sites. Hard work. I saved almost everything I earned. It came in handy when I came down to Montreal to continue with my studies."

Dad looks defensive. "You don't need to go to university to do well. It wouldn't have done me any good."

"Perhaps you didn't have the marks," says Chip provocatively.

Dad glares at him. "Watch out what you're saying. Anyway, you didn't even finish. You quit after your first year."

"After my second year," Chip corrects him.

"What made you move from Montreal back to Goose Bay?" I ask Dad.

"I had this idea of starting my own business. I knew someone up there who could give me a few pointers. That was in '85. At first it went like gangbusters. I sold desks, chairs, all sorts of things to the Government for the schools and hospitals."

"That's also when you married Valérie," adds Chip.

Dad gives Chip a hard look, as if to tell him not to bring up the subject of my mother. "About then."

"But later you moved to Montreal," says Chip.

Dad reflects. "Yes. Then I moved to Montreal."

"Why?" I want to know. "What made you move, Dad?"

He tries to ignore me. "I've done pretty well here. The Steak House, this home."

"Did Mum want to move?" I ask.

Dad looks annoyed. "Yes. She wasn't happy up there.

No-one could speak French. That sort of thing."

"And your business in Goose Bay?" Chip asks.

"It folded," is the reply. "But it didn't take me long before I had started the Steak House in Montreal. That was a good move. It did well once I found the right approach."

"By then I was in Ottawa," Chip remembers, "working for the Government. Do you remember that fight we had when you came up to visit me in Ottawa?" My ears pick up.

Dad shrugs his shoulders. "Do you mean that girl?"

"Yes. Irma. She was really frightened. She actually thought you were going to rape her."

I look at one of them and then at the other. I now see clearly that not far under the surface lies a simmering animosity. "Come on, Chip," Dad says. "I was just being a little friendly. She was asking for it."

Chip is getting red in the face. "Like hell she was asking for it! Not from what she told me. Irma was a soft-mannered girl and whatever it was you did, you were pretty nasty with her. You, a married man. And she was my girlfriend, at least until that happened."

"I don't like your bringing all that up in front of David," Dad says, his eyes narrowing. "Anyway, it's all bullshit." He looks at his watch. "It's getting late. Let's call it a day."

11

The next Tuesday, Chip returns for the reading of the will, and the three of us find ourselves waiting in a rather shabby reception area outside the lawyer's office down on Saint-Antoine street. He comes out to greet us, and Dad introduces Chip and me. The lawyer is wearing a shiny grey suit and a pale blue shirt with an open collar. He is young, but balding. He has acted for Dad before. We all go in and sit down.

"Mr Forbes," he says to Dad. "My condolences. It is sad to lose one's father." He nods to Chip, as if to say the same thing to him. He holds a large brown envelope in his hand. "Shall we proceed?" He opens the envelope and extracts a single sheet of paper with what looks like my grandfather's handwriting on it.

"I shall start," he says, adjusting the reading glasses on his nose. "I, Alexander Leslie Forbes, being of sound mind, hereby make in my own hand this my last will and testament. I leave all of my assets in trust with my executor, to be held and managed by him until my grandson David shall reach the age of thirty, at which time my assets are to be distributed in three equal parts to my son Leo, my son Chipman and my grandson David. My trustee and executor shall have full discretion as to the distribution or accumulation of the revenues from the assets held by him. I hereby name my oldest son Leo as my sole executor and trustee."

The lawyer pauses. "There follows the date and his signature," he says.

I study the faces around me. Dad's is calm and Chip's is puzzled. The lawyer looks slightly nervous; he is staring out the window. "Are there any questions?" he finally asks.

"No," Dad says hastily. "It seems pretty clear. Please make us each a copy and tell us what you have to do to have it verified at court." The lawyer looks at Chip.

"Tell me please," Chip requests. "Are there any witnesses?"

"No," says the lawyer. "It's not necessary when the will is handwritten."

Chip frowns and turns to my father. "When did Dad give you the will? Were you there when he wrote it?"

Dad and the lawyer exchange glances. "No," Dad says. "I wasn't there. He gave it to me later."

Chip seems satisfied, at least for the moment. Nor does he make any comment as we wind matters up with the lawyer and leave his office. It is now mid-afternoon. "I return to Goose Bay tomorrow morning, Leo," he says. "Perhaps we should have a little talk beforehand. May I come around to the house at about seven this evening?"

"Suit yourself," says Dad. "See you then." Chip leaves us, Dad heads for the Steak House and I hurry up the hill to catch my last course of the afternoon. The scene at the lawyer's office lingers in my mind: the reading of the will, Dad's haste in closing off any discussion, the nervous look on the lawyer's face, the terms of the will itself. I sense that trouble may be on its way.

I am also sad to think that Chip is leaving Montreal so quickly; there is so much that we could discuss. I feel drawn to him as I used to be to Grandad. "It will just have to wait," I tell myself.

When I get home after my lecture Dad is waiting for me with a pizza in the oven. "Let's have a quick bite together, David. Then I want you to go out for the evening. Your uncle and I have a few things to discuss together."

I go for a beer with Greg and tell him all about Chip, and about what I have learned from him about my mother. We get quite excited, piecing together the various bits of information.

I also describe the meeting in the lawyer's office. "That will seems cockeyed, Greg. Dad sitting there as trustee of Grandad's money for ten years, doing what he wishes with it."

"It's as though your grandad didn't trust you and wanted to tie things up until you reached thirty."

"But why tie Chip's bit up as well? And Dad's for that matter? No, Greg. The only winner is Dad, who will run Grandad's money for another ten years, with Chip not being able to do anything about it." Greg nods his head in agreement.

The next morning as I am walking to university, my cellphone rings. It is Chip. "David," he says. "I'm at the airport. I wanted to speak to you before returning to Goose Bay. Where are you?"

"Crossing the street." I feel moody and want Chip to realise that I am unhappy that he is disappearing so quickly.

"Look in both directions," he laughs. "Seriously, David. I'm sorry we haven't been able to spend more time together, but you have to understand that I have a job back in Goose Bay, people to talk to, appointments to keep, all that."

"I understand," I say. "Maybe we could spend more time together some other time."

"We'll do that, I promise you. One more thing, David, then I had better run." In the background, I can hear a flight being announced. "I don't want to find myself in a fight with your father and you in the middle. The last thing in the world that I would wish is to make your life with him difficult. However, as I told your father last night, I am deeply disturbed by that will. I doubt its legality and may very well challenge it in court."

I am not surprised by what he says after my discussion with Greg the previous evening. "I understand," is all I choose to say.

"Also, I won't forget my promise to see if I can locate your mother for you."

"Please do. It would mean a lot to me."

"I can believe that. Let's stay in touch. I won't do anything dramatic without telling you. On your part, if ever you want to speak to me, you have my number."

"Thanks, Chip. That's good of you."

He rings off and I walk on in the snow, alone with my thoughts. I feel abandoned. Chip has come and gone. I am left to struggle on, studying for my exams and living with my father. It is then that I remember the documents which were in the shoebox in Grandad's room. "I suppose I should go collect them," I say to myself.

That afternoon, I go to the Residence and ask for Jane.

She arrives at the reception with a large envelope full of Grandad's papers, which she hands over to me. "Your Dad was here the next day," she says with a broad smile. "With another man. They took everything. Lucky we acted first."

After leaving, I call Elka and ask if I can bring the papers over to her home. "Of course," she says. Clearly, her curiosity is aroused.

When I reach her door, it opens immediately. "Quick," she says as she lets me in. The way she shuts the door rapidly behind me, you would think we were in a spy movie. I kick the snow off my boots and remove my coat.

"There's quite a lot in here," I say holding up the envelope. We sit down together in her living room and while she looks on expectantly, I open it and spread its contents over a large coffee table.

In one heap, I place a number of invoices. They appear to relate to various construction jobs that Grandad had up in Labrador in the seventies and eighties, mostly around Nain.

Next, we find my grandmother's birth and death certificates, Grandad's social insurance card and a small bundle of letters. The letters are all in the same handwriting, a woman's hand by the looks of it.

Then comes a legal document, a will. It is typed and signed by Grandad and two witnesses. One witness is the director of the Residence and the other is Jane.

"You had better have a quick look at the will," Elka says. "Just to have a general idea of what's in it. After that, let's make one or two copies." She pours both of us a cup of tea. She is enjoying this. She's no fan of my father and can smell scandal. She is wearing a bright red sweater, and not for the first time I look at her generous breasts and wonder what it would be like to plunge my face between them and feel her soft skin on my cheeks.

Together we read the will. It is on a standard form published by the notarial profession and is very simple: one half of the estate goes outright to Leo and the other half goes outright to Chip, with both named as joint executors. By its date, I can see that it is about five years old.

"So, there are two wills," I say. "The other one is more recent, but my uncle thinks that its validity is questionable."

"You had better tell him about this one then. What would make the other one invalid?"

I pull out my phone and dial the number for Chip's cellphone. "Let's ask him."

Chip is in an airport lounge somewhere and answers at once. "Chip," I say excitedly. "It's David. I've just found a second will."

"Aha!" he exclaims. "Where did you find it?"

"It was in Grandad's papers at the Residence. I went there just now to pick them up."

"What's its date? Is it earlier or later than the handwritten one?"

"Earlier." I tell him the date. "It is printed on some kind of form and witnessed. In it, everything is left to you and Dad in equal shares."

"Who is the executor?"

I look to be sure. "You and Dad are joint executors." I am beginning to feel excited at my discovery. "Which will is the good one, Chip? Why do you think the other one that the lawyer has may not be valid?"

"Because Grandad had to be in good mental health to make a valid will. 'Of sound mind' is the expression. He also had to do it of his free will. It just doesn't make sense that he would have left everything in trust like that."

Chip's voice changes: it sounds tense, a bit hard. "David, the will you found is very important. I think the other one, the one the lawyer read to us, is a goddam fraud." His voice chokes on these last words. "I'm sorry, David. I got a bit carried away there. Forget what I just said. Would you mind sending me a copy of the will you just found?"

"Certainly, Chip. I'll do so right away."

"Don't go away," he says hurriedly. "I have a couple of questions. Tell me how you found Grandad over the past year or two? Was he always rational, always lucid?"

"No," I say. "He was very forgetful and seemed confused. He hasn't been one hundred percent for three or four years now."

"Thanks, David. You may have to repeat that to a judge one day. I'll try as hard as I can to avoid that. Clearly, though, the handwritten will was made at a time when your grandfather was no longer sound of mind. It's more than likely that Leo dictated it to him, possibly with help from that lawyer of his." I hear a lot of noise in the background. "Got to run, David," he says. "Goodbye for now."

"Goodbye, Chip." I ring off and summarise the conversation for Elka.

She and I then return to my grandad's papers, and I pick up the bundle of letters. "You should read them first yourself," she says to me. "They may be personal. They look it anyway." She leaves me sitting there and I open the bundle. There are seven letters in all, dated from 1983 to 1987, that is, starting about four years after my grandmother's death when Grandad was in his late fifties and still living in Nain. The handwriting is very neat and precise and appears to be that of a woman. All are simply signed "M".

The first is brief. In it, the writer thanks my grandfather for his kindness in sending her a package of books. "I left them on the big table at the school library, and they were an immediate success. We badly needed a few new books. Thank you so much."

The second is dated May 1985. "Today, the ice started to break up in the bay. The geese were restless, and more and more were arriving in great flights from the south. How is it in Nain? When will I see you again?"

The third and fourth were both in November 1986. They dealt largely with plans for M's visit to Goose Bay in her capacity as a teacher at the school in Hopedale. In the second one there is a telling passage. "Thank you for your kind words. I sometimes ask myself what is the most important thing in my life. Your letters are the answer, at least when we are not together. You are my eagle."

In the fifth one, dated January, 1987, M seems to refer to an argument between them. "I am so sorry. I don't know why I said what I did. Please understand me, we are very different from each other. We don't always think the same way, and you must forgive me."

The last two are dated 1987, but without a precise date. In one M writes about a forest fire that seems to have threatened Hopedale for a while, but then was extinguished by the rain. "The smoke was annoying, but thankfully it only went on for a day or so."

The other letter, M's last, seems to refer to some external event that is cause for their ceasing, or at least interrupting, their relationship. "I have read your letter. What happened is so sad, so horrible, that I don't know what to say. I need some time to think it over. Let's not see each other for now. Please understand me. Yours ever."

I carefully return all the papers to their envelope and sit there in thought.

12

"Rinnnnnng! Rinnnnnng!" The silence of the night is shattered by the telephone, which sits on a table in the hall outside my bedroom. I am startled, and the Statistics notes in my lap fall to the floor. I can hear Dad stumbling and swearing as he leaves his room to pick up the phone.

It is one twenty-five in the morning, very late for a phone call. There must be an emergency; something bad must have happened. I go out to the landing just in time to see Dad racing past me down the stairs. "Fire! David. Fire! There's a fire over at the Steak House."

After he leaves, I put my notes away, turn out the lights and try going to sleep. Without success. Grandad's funeral and Chip's visits are only three weeks past and are too fresh in my mind. So are all my difficulties with Dad. I try sleeping on one side and am driven crazy by a pounding noise in my ear. I try the other side, and for some reason or other my shoulder feels sore. When I hear Dad opening the front door of the house at four-thirty or so, and stamping the snow off his boots, I still am awake.

"A total loss, David," he laments. "The kitchen, the

dining area, the reception, all destroyed. What a disaster."
He sits down on a chair in the hall and buries his face in
his hands. He appears exhausted, and more than a bit
emotional.

I try to comfort him and fetch him a whisky, which
he really appreciates and probably needs. We wait there
wordlessly as he drains his glass. "We can talk tomorrow,"
he finally says. "I'm bushed. I need some sleep."

Four or five hours later, we are seated at the kitchen
table facing each other. "It shouldn't have happened," he
says. "I think the cook must have left something on in the
kitchen. That dumb bastard. I keep telling him to check
everything, but he never does." I top up his coffee and he
continues.

"You can't trust anyone anymore, Davie. It's a bugger.
No one is reliable. The only person you can rely on is
yourself. That goddamn cook!"

"Have you spoken to him?" I ask.

"Not yet, but he'll never admit to anything. He's that
way. And the fire department has left the place in such
a shambles we'll never know what happened. What a
destructive bunch! They smashed the front window, then
the reception area. One wall of the kitchen, they more or
less chopped down. There's water everywhere. Oh my
God! What'll I do?" He throws up his hands and gives a
deep sigh. I feel really sorry for him.

"David." He looks at me intently, draining his cup of
coffee. "You have got to understand. There will probably
be an enquiry. Standard procedure. The police have to
prepare a report. So do the insurers. I just want it to be
clear in your mind that I was here all yesterday evening
with you in the house."

I look at him and at first say nothing. Then I sort of
nod my agreement. However, as what he is requesting

sinks in, I get a funny feeling in my stomach. It is not at all clear in my mind that Dad was in the house all the previous evening. I came home at the usual hour and went straight to my room. He might have been there at the time, but I didn't see him. I studied until very late, but all the while my door was closed. I don't know where he was. Is he expecting me to say something, possibly even to lie, just to save his skin?

He leaves me with no opportunity to protest. "That's a good boy," he says. "I know I can rely on you. Now excuse me, I think I'll have a good shower and then get a bit more sleep."

Over the next few days, although I keep expecting to be contacted by the police or the insurers, nothing of the sort occurs. However, when I am discussing the fire with Elka she tells me that in the news they say that on the night of the fire someone looking like my father was seen in the vicinity of the Steak House an hour or so after it closed. This makes me extremely worried. It would be awful if it turned out that Dad actually started the fire himself in order to collect insurance or for some other such reason.

One evening after a game of squash, Greg and I have a late bite at a tavern near home. "It's a bummer," I say to him. "What if I am asked questions about where Dad was the night of the fire?"

"Just say you don't know."

"Yes, but even that could contradict something that he has already said. For example, he may have said that we spent the evening together watching TV. You see the problem?"

Greg chuckles. "Yes, but surely it's his problem."

"I think that with the will and now the fire, Dad is storing up some big problems for himself." I put down my glass of draught beer. "Tell me, Greg. Do you ever want people to have problems just because you think that they will have problems?"

"I don't follow."

"Well, if you foresee an event, you naturally expect it to happen. What can be nasty, in particular if the event will not be a happy one, is when you actually begin to hope that it will happen."

Greg nods. "It's just vanity. We want events to prove us right."

"Yes, and I am beginning to feel this way about Dad. Rationally, I shouldn't wish him bad luck. It's not in my interest. However, I can see that he may be heading for trouble, in one form or another. Despite myself, I am beginning to look for signs of that trouble, and worse still, to wish for them. I'm not proud of the fact, but that's the way it is. In effect, I hope Dad gets his comeuppance. My own father!"

One day in late March, I leave home and move in with Elka, bless her. She sets up a bed for me in my study room at the back of her apartment. I cart my belongings down below in the afternoon when Dad is away at work. On his return I speak to him. "Dad. I am finding it difficult living here and studying below. I spend my whole time running back and forth. In any event my friends all live on their own. I'm about the only one who still lives at home. I hope you don't mind. I'm moving down to Elka's."

As I talk, he has been shifting his jaw back and forth as if he was chewing something. "David." He speaks slowly. "I don't think that's a very good idea."

"I won't be far away," I say, with an attempt at a smile. The tension is rising between us.

"You'll be cramped. It's pretty small down there and that woman talks a lot. She'll drive you nuts."

"We get along just fine," I say. "In fact, I've already

moved, Dad. Let me try it out for a while."

He scowls. "You don't seem to be giving me much of a choice."

"It's not very far. I'll stay in touch."

"Your room will still be here for you if you change your mind. Any time." He says this ungraciously. If anything, I am confirmed in my decision.

Over the following weeks, I go upstairs to visit him from time to time. I tell him that I am studying hard, which pleases him. He occasionally tries to get me to change my mind, but eventually gives up. For my part, I realise just how stressful it was for me living with him. Now I am more relaxed and find it easier to concentrate on my books.

13

It is on a blustery winter day in early April that Chip calls me. His voice is exultant, trembling with emotion. "David. I just spoke to her. Valérie. Your mother. She's in good health and living in Baie- Comeau. She was overwhelmed. She wants to see you."

The biggest dream of my life suddenly seems to be on the point of coming true. I am completely taken by surprise. "Where did you say she is? Is she well? What did she say?"

"Baie-Comeau, David. She lives in Baie-Comeau. When I called, I started by saying who I was. That took a while. She kept interrupting me. She wanted to know why I was calling. From where? At first, she was very suspicious. I think that she was afraid that your father and I were acting together."

"Did she ask about me?"

"That came next. Once I had convinced her that I wasn't in cahoots with your father, I said that I had met with you. Then came a whole new burst of questions. How did we come to meet? Where were you? Were you living with Leo? What were you doing? What were you like? It took me a while to explain all that. I had to go over it several times."

As I listen, a great joy is coming over me. The feeling is indescribable. It is as though I have just got out of prison or discovered a new planet. "Does she want to see me?"

"Of course she does, but she doesn't want your father to know. She said, 'I absolutely don't want to have anything to do with Leo.' She then made a funny noise. I think that she was in tears."

"When can I see her?"

"As soon as you can get to Baie-Comeau."

The big day is set for the following Saturday. I will travel by bus and will leave Montreal on Friday afternoon. Chip will join up with me in Baie-Comeau.

From the time of Chip's call, I count the hours and can think of nothing else. On Wednesday and Thursday nights I hardly get any sleep. Chip sends me the bus ticket, I print it and put it in my wallet. Then I keep taking it out to make sure that it is there, and to verify the hour of departure. I must look a thousand times at the photo I found in Grandad's room, wondering what my mother will look like now. I even discuss the whole business with my Inuit carving, which sits on the desk where I study as a sort of companion with whom I can carry out imagined conversations. "What'll she be like?" I ask it. "Wait and see," is the answer.

My big problem during this period is what to say to my father if I should meet him. I still have to go upstairs to my former room to fetch clothes and the like. Fortunately, he is always out when I go, and I am able to leave him a note on the kitchen table saying that my studies are going well and that I plan to pass the weekend with some friends.

On Friday, I go to the bus terminal in Montreal over

an hour early.

When I finally take my seat at the front of the bus, just behind the driver, I'm a wreck. As we pull out of the terminal it starts to snow and the going is slow. Staring out the window at Montreal's endless suburbs buried in snow, and soothed by the windshield wipers of the bus as they flick back and forth, I feel my eyelids growing heavy and fall into a deep sleep.

In Quebec City, I am obliged to wait in the terminal and then take a second bus. It doesn't matter to me as long as I am on my way. I am as in a dream, time is suspended. I have never been east of Quebec in my entire life. We pass through one town after another, all with names that are familiar to me, but none of which I have ever seen before. The distances between stops become longer and longer. The piles of snow get higher and higher and the trees get shorter and shorter. I sustain myself with chocolate bars and packets of nuts.

I have my moments of doubt as well. What if I don't like her? What if she doesn't turn out to be like the person I have started to imagine in my mind? Perhaps I am not going to please her. What if we are unable to love each other as we should?

When the driver finally announces that we are to arrive at Baie-Comeau in twenty minutes' time it comes as a complete shock, and my adrenaline starts to race.

Chip is waiting for me at the bus stop. He waves at me energetically as I climb down from the bus. "Nervous?" he grins. "You look a wreck. You had better go inside the terminal and wash up a bit."

As we drive through Baie-Comeau, I look at my uncle out of the corner of my eye. I am struck by his energy and calm self-confidence. He looks to be a man who is *bien dans sa peau*, at ease with himself. It is something that

I envy. I hope one day to be like that! At the same time, I feel a touch of guilt stealing away from my father without letting him know what is going on.

Chip pulls a slip of paper out of his pocket. "Twenty-four, David. We want number twenty-four."

"Twenty-one," I read on a door. "It must be on the other side. Park anywhere here, Chip. We can easily walk." I can't wait to get out of the car.

There it is: number twenty-four! I jump out of the car and leap over a snowbank at the side of the road. In front of me is an outdoors wooden staircase which I take two steps at a time before ringing the bell. My heart is pounding.

Almost immediately, the door swings open. There in the doorway stands a tall, sturdy woman with semi-blonde hair in her late forties. She is wearing a rust-coloured cardigan over a yellow turtle-necked sweater and a tweed skirt. She is smiling and laughing, and I particularly notice her teeth, which are very even and white.

"David!" she exclaims, pronouncing my name in the French manner and reaching out to me. She wraps me tightly in her arms and holds me there for the longest of times. I can feel her body heaving and realise that she is sobbing. "Mother!" I say slightly awkwardly, repeating it several times. I find myself smothered in her embrace and can smell her hair and feel her softness.

Then comes a moment when I hesitate and draw back. I need to collect my thoughts. What do I know about this woman who is my mother, but whom I have never truly met before? She reads my mind and draws back as well. She places her hands on my shoulders and gives me a warm smile. "David. We must take all the time we need to get to know each other. Let's not rush it. But believe me, David, this is the happiest day of my life. Honestly."

Her smile causes little wrinkles to appear about her

eyes. I notice her nose, which is strong, and her jaw, that suggests determination. I feel her warmth entering into me.

We are still on the doorstep of her home and I can hear Chip behind me, stamping his boots to knock the snow off. "Brrr," she says to us. "Come on in, both of you. It's freezing out here."

We go inside, where we are greeted by a blast of warm air. She closes the door behind us and reaches out her hand to Chip, who shakes it. He looks taken aback; I think he expected them to exchange a kiss on the cheek. All the same, he manages a cheerful smile. "Well, Valérie, this is certainly a special occasion. I must say you are looking wonderful."

She returns his smile rapidly and turns away to show us a cupboard by the door. "Put your coats here. Have you come all the way from Montréal, David? Chip said you were intending to take the bus. *Pauvre petit. Tu dois être épuisé.*"

We sit down for a cup of tea in the living room. It is tastefully decorated, sunny and welcoming. I glance at the bookshelves and recognise the names of a number of French authors. My mother has prepared a number of small sandwiches, which I attack with zeal.

"David," she says to me. "There you are my own flesh and blood!" She pauses and directs a careful smile at me. "Are you happy to discover your mother?"

"Mother," I manage to say. "This is the biggest day in my life, but I don't quite know what to say. You'll have to forgive me."

"Yes," she agrees. "This is a big day for both of us, but it is also a complicated one. We have so many things to say to each other. A lot of years have gone by, a lot of things have happened. Much needs to be explained."

I think of this for a while, trying to find a place to start. "Why?" I ask her. "How come this happened to us?"

My mother shakes her head. "It shouldn't have happened, I know. I let you down, David. I failed you. I just hope you will forgive me when I explain all of the circumstances to you."

I quickly seek to reassure her. "I should have tried harder to find you too, Mother. Let's not start looking for someone to blame."

"Tell me about your life in Montreal," she says. "That's what I want to hear about."

I describe for her Dad's house, my school and later studies, my friends, the Steak House, the outings with Dad on Lac Saint-Louis, all that. She asks me particularly about my marks at university. She then wants to know my feelings about Dad.

I am careful in my answer. I am not comfortable taking sides between my parents. "He has been kind to me. But it has never been what I would call a warm relationship. Somehow, it's as though I am there so he does the necessary. There are also times when I feel that he is trying to control me. And he has always refused to talk to me about you."

She looks at me sharply. "As if I didn't exist?"

"Precisely. More than once, I have tried to find out about you, where you live, how I might contact you. Each time, he becomes angry, calls you names and refuses to answer. It is only thanks to Chip that we are here together today."

She looks gratefully at Chip. "Yes, we owe you a lot, Chip. You have my thanks." She then turns back to me. "What you say doesn't surprise me, David. Leo was like that with me also. He always wanted to control me, to decide himself what I should know and what I should not know. Tell me, does he live with a woman? Someone who has acted a bit as a mother for you?"

"No," I answer simply. "We have lived together all these years just the two of us, Dad and I. Recently, I moved out of the house. I'm now living in the basement flat with a neighbour who has always been very kind to me. An older woman named Elka."

"I see. What made you move out?"

"Oh, a number of things, Mother." I tell her of my increasing difficulties with Dad, of Grandad's death, of the matter of the two wills, and finally of the Steak House fire. When I am finished, she turns to Chip.

"What do you think, Chip? Is Leo playing games?"

Chip sighs. "Leo was never the easiest person to get along with, Valérie. I certainly think that the second will is fishy. As for the fire, who knows? It may be fishy too."

My mother nods. "It wouldn't surprise me." She turns to me. "Tell me more about your grandfather. Were you close to him?"

"Yes, very close," I answer. "He lived near us in a senior's residence. I used to visit him, we got along very well together. In some ways he was a second father to me."

"Your grandfather was a good man," my mother says. "He and I always saw eye to eye."

This makes me think of the photograph in my wallet, and I pull it out to show her. "Look, Mother. Here is a photo that Grandad kept in his papers. It obviously meant a lot to him."

My mother looks at it closely. "I have never seen it before." She gives a bitter laugh. "We looked a very happy family, didn't we? I'm afraid it didn't last long." She looks at the inscription on the back. "I wonder who took the picture. I don't recognise the handwriting."

Chip and I both have a look. "I don't recognise it

either," Chip says. "That looks more like a woman's hand. Dad's writing was pretty messy and microscopic, as though he was trying to save on the paper." We all have a little laugh.

My mother then quizzes me on my plans to go to medical school. Clearly, she approves. "David. You can be proud of yourself. Good going." A curious sadness comes over us at this point. It is as if we regret the lost years, she of being my mother and I, of being her son.

Chip senses the uncertain mood and rises to his feet. "Come on, you two! Stop moping! Let's celebrate. This is a happy occasion, not a wake. We need some champagne! Where can I find some, Val?" It is as though he half expects her to have a bottle ready in the fridge.

"At the SAQ," my mother says. Taking Chip to the window, she points down the street. "Do you see where that blue car is parked? That's Cartier Street. Turn left there and go two blocks. The store is on your right." Chip puts on his boots and coat and heads out the door.

I stay on with Mother and we continue to tell each other about ourselves and about the lives that we have been living. "Getting through the divorce was the worst thing that I have ever had to do in my life," she tells me. "It was a long and bitter struggle. I tried to be reasonable, but Leo was very aggressive, almost vindictive."

"Were you living in Montreal at the time?" I ask.

"Yes, but when we separated, I returned to Baie-Comeau. I had no money, so I took a job as a waitress in a company cafeteria. Not long after that I had a nervous breakdown and lost my job. I also became anaemic. One of my brothers stepped in and found me a spot in a sort of convalescence home. I stayed there for quite some time. It took me about three years to find my feet again."

"Where was I all that time?" I ask.

"With Leo. At the beginning, I wanted to have you come with me, but Leo refused and I just didn't have the strength to fight it out. That's when I became ill. I'm sorry, David, I know it wasn't right, but you can't imagine how bad I was at the time. I was constantly on sedatives. It was a fight for survival."

"What did you do when you got over your illness?" I ask.

"I returned to my studies and obtained my teacher's certificate. That is something that I'm really proud of. It was my way back, my way out of depression. I took a teaching job with the local school board, here in Baie-Comeau. I still teach there. I teach French literature."

"That explains all the books," I say admiringly, looking at the crowded shelves behind where we are seated.

Mother gives a short smile. "Please believe me, David, I was so ashamed at having abandoned you. I thought about you all the time. At one point, I found out where you were living with Leo and tried to make contact. By now, you would have been about six or seven years old. At first, Leo didn't return my calls. Finally, we spoke and he agreed to meet me in Quebec City to talk things over."

"Why in Quebec?" I ask.

"He didn't want me to go all the way to Montreal. He pretended that you would be with him in Quebec, but he tricked me. When we met in a shabby restaurant near the bus station, he was alone and in one of his moods. He told me that if I ever tried to see you, he would kill you. Not me, but you. Those were his very words."

I try to imagine the scene. Dad threatening my mother like that. To kill me. Would he have done so? Was he that bad?

"I was shattered," Mother continued. "But I knew what he was capable of. I believed him." Mother is looking pale. She is twisting a tissue in her hands and holding the tears back. "I apologise, David. I wanted to see you so much, you can't imagine. But what was I to do?"

She rises and clears a few plates away. I can hear her blowing her nose in the kitchen, and go to the window to see if Chip has reappeared. "David," she says urgently from the door of the kitchen. "Leo mustn't find out that we have met. At least not right away. You won't tell him, will you?"

"No, Mother," I reply. "Not until we figure out a good way to break it to him."

My mother returns to the living room with three champagne glasses and joins me at the window. "Here comes Chip," she says. "What do you think of him? He's a nice man, isn't he? Very different from Leo. They don't even look like each other, except the nose I suppose."

"I like him a lot," I say spontaneously. "We're becoming very friendly. I hope it will continue like that. It's good having someone I can turn to."

My mother smiles at me. "You can count on me now as well."

We hear Chip at the front door, then he bursts into the room waving a bottle in his hand and the three of us crowd around as he opens the champagne and pours us each a glass. My mother proposes the toast. "To you, David. May you and I never be separated again, and may your life be a good one and a happy one." She takes a sip and sinks back into an armchair. She suddenly looks exhausted.

"Well, David," Chip says a few minutes later as we leave Mother's home. "What do you make of all that?"

"I..." The words aren't coming to me. "She's a wonderful woman," I manage to say. There is a lump in my throat, and my voice sounds strange to me.

We get in the car. "She was looking a bit tired at the

end," he says. "That was a lot for her, remembering Leo, meeting you. It was also a lot for you. I know a place where we can have a decent meal. Then you should have a good night's sleep. I told your mother that we would return to see her tomorrow at eleven."

Once we are at our table, I tell Chip of my conversation with Mother while he was off buying the wine. "Dad told her that he would kill me if she tried to see me. Do you think that he would have done that?"

Chip shakes his head. "David. As I remember him, your father is a man with a fair temper. He can be rash and impetuous, and say things that he doesn't mean. No. I don't think that he would have killed his own son. All the same, he might have done something that wasn't pleasant. I can understand your mother's fear."

"Mum told me that she was very ill after the divorce." I pause and realise that I have just called my mother '*Mum*'. The sound is wonderful to my ears. 'Mum'. I have a 'Mum'. A warm sensation sweeps over me.

"What illness?" Chip asks.

"She had a nervous breakdown, or something like that." I think a bit. "Yes, and anaemia. She told me that she had anaemia. Then when she was better, she tried to get in touch with me and that's when Dad threatened to kill me. She is very anxious that he not learn about our present visit," I add.

"I'm sure she's right," Chip says pensively. "There are a lot of destabilising things happening in your father's life right now. Your grandad's death and the matter of his estate, the Steak House fire, your moving out of the house. Yes. It would be far better that he not learn about your meeting up with your mother, but he will have to do so one day or another. It's going to be tricky."

We finish our meal and go back to the hotel where we

are sharing a room. As I get into bed, I call over to Chip. "Thanks, Chip. Thanks for everything. You've been great."

"Not at all," he replies. "Get some sleep now. You must be tired, and if you're not, I sure am!"

14

The next morning finds us back at my mother's door. It is not intended to be a long visit, as my bus for Montreal leaves in the early afternoon and Chip will have a long drive back to Goose Bay. My mother welcomes us with warmth and we each get a hug and a kiss. All the same, she seems distracted. I sense that something is on her mind.

We start out by discussing the life that Chip has led. My mother asks him a number of questions. We hear about his work for the Canadian Government. He tells us how he loves the solitude of the north and is never happier than when he is in a canoe or behind a dogsled. He has never married, at least not formally.

We then discuss my father again, and my mother makes Chip promise not to speak to him of our visit with her. I wonder how we can really do that. "I want to be able to have a normal relationship with you, Mum. I want to visit you often, to get to know you better. How can I possibly do that and keep it all a secret?"

"David is right, Valérie," Chip adds. "We're going to have to break it to him somehow."

"Then let's do it gradually," my mother says. "First, David says he's visiting you, Chip, and Leo gets used to that idea. Then later on I enter into the picture." We settle on this as the best plan.

Then my mother drops her bombshell. "David. There is something that I have struggled with all my life." She pauses. "Something I have difficulty even admitting to myself. But now that we have met, I think I must tell it to you. I was thinking about it all last night. It is so very important that I have no choice. It is going to change everything for you, so you had better prepare yourself."

She looks at me with a strange intensity. I have become enchanted by the sound of my mother's voice. There is an unusual mellowness to it. It is a voice full of kindness. At present however, it becomes oddly toneless and emotionless, almost as though she is under hypnosis. She darts a nervous glance at Chip. He appears unconcerned. This is something between Mum and me.

"When Leo and I were first married," she starts, "we lived in Goose Bay. Leo had his business and things were fine. He was handsome then and could be very charming."

"I loved him at first. I really did. Then he began looking at other women. He became unfaithful. Our relationship started unravelling in front of my eyes. I protested, and that made matters worse. He became violent. Yes. Violent with me."

My mother's voice has become lower, and I have to listen hard to hear everything.

"At a certain point in time, we moved to Montreal. I never fully understood why and was certainly not consulted. Your grandad came down from Nain to visit us and say goodbye. Leo closed his business, and in no time, we were gone."

"Things were no better between us when we got to

Montreal, although at least Leo was pretty tied up trying to start a new business. He was often away though, chasing skirts at least some of the time, I am sure. Our life as a couple stopped completely, unless you call the occasional argument part of one's life as a couple." She shrugs. "That's not my idea of marriage in any event." She then turns to Chip and visibly takes a deep breath.

"Do you remember, Chip, the time you visited us when Leo and I had borrowed that chalet in the Laurentians?"

Chip looks at my mother and his eyes widen. I think he may be signalling to her to stop. He clears his throat. "Yes, Valérie," he states slowly. "I remember the time I visited you in the Laurentians."

"Leo went off to see some lady friend. I was furious with him. He told me he would meet me back in Montreal." I look from my mother to Chip and back again. They both appear nervous.

My mother's voice is strained. "David. I am about to make you an admission. I wish I didn't have to; really, I do. However, it is the only proper thing for me to do."

She pauses to choose her words, and then speaks rapidly. "Chip and I spent the night together. It was entirely my doing." She looks at Chip. He shrugs silently and shifts uncomfortably in his chair. For my part I am baffled. I can't see why all of a sudden my mother has decided to tell me this.

"Believe me, David," my mother adds. "We hadn't done it before, and we have not done it since."

Chip is hanging onto her every word, clearly not knowing what will come next. "I'm sorry, Val. I really am."

My mother is now close to tears. She holds her hand up. "Wait!" She looks intensely at me. "David, there is a reason why I am telling you this." I feel my face getting redder and redder even though I don't know why.

"David. You were born more or less nine months after that night."

I am so startled that at first, my mind simply stops functioning. Then the implications start to register. I begin to see my whole life turning upside down. "What? What?" I look at her and then at Chip, who has raised his hand to his forehead and shut his eyes.

"David." She continues. "A woman knows. She doesn't make any mistakes about these things. David, my darling David, my long-lost David, my dearest David." She seizes my hand. "Leo is not your father, Chip is." Chip and I look at each other in astonishment, and my mother bursts into tears.

15

I chew on my pencil and stare out the window of the back room in Elka's apartment.

Leo is not your father, Chip is.

The words are burning in my brain. They are ringing constantly in my ears. They are words that I shall remember for the rest of my life.

Two pigeons are bobbing back and forth on the sill outside, cooing noisily to each other. It's hard to concentrate, and my exams are coming closer and closer. I swear at the pigeons and shoo them away through the glass pane. In doing so, I hit my textbook on anatomy and it flips shut so that I lose my place. "Merde!"

Leo is not your father, Chip is.

Who am I then? What have I been doing all my life? The house I was brought up in now seems an accident that did not have to happen. The school that I went to as well, the street, the neighbourhood, even my father Leo. I am not his son at all. I am the son of a completely different person, whom I barely know. In a sense my past is simply erased. I am without a past.

The person I am, my personality, these too are grounded in falsity. My life with Leo has surely had a big influence on me. How would I be if I hadn't lived all that time with him, but rather with Chip? Perhaps I would never have lived in Montreal, but rather in Ottawa, and then the far north. I would not have gone to the same school, had the same friends. I would be unable to speak French. I would be a different person.

In addition, I am beginning to ask myself what kind of a screwed-up family I come from, where one brother tries to seduce the other brother's girlfriend and then the other brother sleeps with the first brother's wife. I wonder if Chip felt guilty about his little transgression, if that was why he disappeared up to Hudson Bay. Did Leo suspect something, and is that why our relationship has always been so complicated?

It is hard, if not impossible, to separate the strands of what was from what might have been. The result is a confused tangle vibrating in my mind. I no longer am sure of who I am or where I am going.

I get up and go into Elka's kitchen to make myself a cup of coffee. "This must stop," I say to myself, "or I will flunk for sure." With a superhuman effort, I return to my desk with coffee in hand and find the place in my book where I left off.

Day after day, the same scenario is repeated. Day after day, my exams come closer.

I fall into the habit of speaking to my little Inuit head, sitting nearby on my desk or on the windowsill like a mascot. Each time it makes me think of the Inuit girl I met years before at the hostel. A link has been established there that I do not wish to break. She is becoming the girl of my dreams, a goddess embodied in that little sculpture. It is all ridiculous, I know, but thinking of this almost imaginary girl with her black braids and special eyes somehow permits me to forget about the rest and get on with my studies.

Chip calls me regularly on the phone. At first, he is nervous, and in fact we both are. He understands that these new developments in my life have unsettled me, and we discuss them at length. I find this very helpful, and gradually return to an easier frame of mind. He has invited me to spend the summer with him in Labrador once I am finished with exams. It's tempting, but if I do decide to go, I will have to break the news to Dad.

I also speak occasionally to Mum, and between us the conversations are very careful. I think it is because what we have to say to each other is very intimate, and I am not good at being intimate. It just isn't me. I suppose that over the years I have built up too many defences.

I also visit Leo, my erstwhile father. I try to make idle conversation, avoiding anything that might touch on Chip or my mother. These visits are particularly difficult, as I now view our relationship through an entirely new prism. He is no longer my father. I no longer owe him the duty of a son to a father. I do owe him some gratitude for what he has done for me, but at the same time I am now free to pass judgement. Shouldn't he have simply turned me over to my mother and let me be brought up by her?

I badly need to discuss my new circumstances with someone, but with whom? I decide not Elka, as she knows my father and lives just next door to him. Gregory for sure. But somehow, Irene keeps coming to mind, so one Saturday, I go looking for her at the hour when her hair salon usually closes for the day.

There she is drying someone's hair. It seems her work is almost over, and I wait outside in the street until she eventually appears. She grabs my arm. "I'm really happy to see you again, David. Where are you going to take me? It's cold out here. Let's go for a coffee." It feels good to be together again.

We go to one of our old haunts and find our favourite table, empty and waiting for us. We order two Irish coffees. "What's your news, David? When are exams?"

"Well, my first exam is the week after next, but let's have your news first," I say. "When are you going to get married?"

She replies with gusto. "It's off. Finito! Kaput!"

This I did not expect. But with Irene... "What happened?" I ask.

"I decided I wanted to keep my independence. Simple as that. We still see each other, but I don't want anyone else to tell me what to do."

Her words don't seem to invite any further comment, and again she asks me for my news. She quizzes me so effectively that I find myself telling her about how I have met my mother, who is wonderful, and how - under sworn secrecy - I have discovered that Leo is not my real father, and how my real father is my uncle, the one who was at the funeral, and who seems pretty nice...

"Wow!" she exclaims. "It's just like Paolo and Francesca."

"Paolo and who?" I ask. Sometimes Irene really astonishes me. This time it's no exception. She stands up in the café, spreads her arms out wide, and in an attempt to imitate a man's voice declaims to everyone in the café

"amor ch'a nullo amato amar perdona."

I look about, startled and embarrassed. A number of people have looked up, but no one seems to care. "Irene. Please sit down," I tug at her sleeve. "What on earth are you talking about?"

"Dad used to recite it to us," she explains, as she regains her chair. "He could go on for quite a few lines. Shall I tell you the story?"

Irene is a real tonic. When she gets going, all my worries melt away. "Please do," I answer readily.

"It comes from Dante's Divine Comedy. Francesca was really pretty. Her parents arranged for her to marry a nobleman called Gianciotto. At least, I think that was his name. But she didn't understand and thought that she was marrying his younger brother Paolo. It seems that the older brother was really ugly, and the younger one really good-looking. After she married the older one, she was unhappy and made a pass at Paolo." Irene pauses for effect, leans towards me and puts her hand on my shoulder. Her voice has now dropped to a dramatic whisper.

"One day, she and Paolo are screwing in the palazzo on a stone bench near the window. The older brother comes along. He can see what's going on, even under all those clothes that they used to wear. He gets really mad. You see," she pauses. "It's a bit like your father and your uncle."

"There are parallels," I say. "What happened next? I'm all ears."

"Yep!" She looks me straight in the eye. "Get prepared. The older brother ran the two of them through with his sword. He skewered them there together, just like a kebab."

The way she says it, I can almost feel the blade sliding through me. "Irene!" I protest.

"That's more or less like Dante tells it. Read it for

yourself." We have a good laugh together and I feel a lot better, even if the image of Paolo and Francesca skewered together does remain with me for some time.

16

The next day it is raining cats and dogs, and Greg and I are sitting in the sunroom of his parents' country house on Covey Hill. He is listening to me calmly, like a psychiatrist would, I suppose. Outside, a small group of cattle drift placidly across our line of vision, their red coats stained dark in the rain. They are following a large green tractor. In it is Greg's dad, taking them a round bale of hay.

I have just told Greg about my trip to Baie-Comeau, meeting my mother at long last, and discovering that my uncle Chip is almost certainly my biological father. Greg is intrigued, and can't avoid a bit of a laugh at my expense.

"He seems like a good guy, at least what I saw of him at the funeral."

"He is. We've been talking a lot on the phone, and so far we get along fine. He's cheerful and kind, and I feel I can trust what he says."

"Your father, Leo I mean, is going to find all this a bitter pill to swallow."

"You can say that again. It's really awkward going to see him nowadays. I don't feel the same way about him anymore. It's as though he has become a different person."

"Do you think it shows? Do you think he suspects something?"

"No. I suppose we were drifting apart already before all this came along. Now, however, the gap is widening rapidly. At least for me it is."

"What do you talk about when you see each other?"

"He keeps bringing up the same old subjects: Grandad's will, the Steak House fire, my duties as his son. He quizzes me as well, tries to get me to talk, but I don't know what he's looking for."

"Fishing. He's fishing."

"I guess so. Trying to find out if I know something he doesn't want me to know. Just what, I don't know, but something important." Greg nods.

"For example," I explain, "when they were first married, he and Mum lived in Goose Bay. He had a business there. Then he suddenly closed the business and they moved to Montreal, where I was born. What made them move? Mum doesn't know to this day. Why do you suppose he would do something like that?"

"Then he always goes back to Grandad and Labrador. What did Grandad tell me about his life up there? Did he ever show me papers or things he had brought with him from up there?"

"Oh! And there is another thing I haven't told you. Elka says she was out of her apartment a few weeks back, and when she returned, she had the feeling that someone had been in her home. Just a feeling. She checked all over, and nothing was missing. It makes me think of the time I found Dad rummaging through my room."

"Does he have a key to her home?"

"Yes. They each keep a key for the other, as a service really. In case one of them loses his key. Elka is convinced it was Dad. Happily, I had put my Inuit head back in its hiding place. I sometimes wonder if that's what he's looking for. But why?"

The rain has stopped, and we step outside avoiding the puddles. A few hens wander by on the lawn looking for fresh worms. Kate the border collie sits nearby, watching attentively as Greg's dad parks the tractor beside the barn.

"When are you going to tell Leo that you have met your mother?" Greg asks.

"My mother wants us to wait. She feels that we should start out by getting him used to the idea that Chip and I are seeing each other. This will happen soon, as I hope to spend the summer in Goose Bay. I haven't told Dad yet, but I'm going to have to one of these days."

"Tell me more about Chip," Greg says. "If Leo had something to hide, would Chip know about it?"

"No, I doubt that. If so, he would tell me. He saw very little of my parents, Leo and Valérie I mean, once he moved to Ottawa. That must have been before they split up, and certainly before I was born."

The ground is so wet, it's steaming, and we return inside.

"There's something else, Greg. Back about fifteen years ago my mother met my Dad in Quebec City, and he told her that if she ever tried to get in touch with me, he would kill me."

"Kill her, you mean."

"No, no. Me."

"That's weird. Really strange. Do you think he actually meant it? Fathers don't usually kill their sons."

"Chip had the same reaction. He thinks it was just bluster."

As I am saying this it suddenly dawns on me that Chip's reasoning no longer holds. Leo may not yet be

aware of it, but I am not his son! A chill runs down my
back at the thought.

17

"Welcome to Goose Bay," Chip calls out with a grin. "The end of the line! Wonderful to see you, David."

"Good to be here," I answer, looking around me. My first impression of Goose Bay is one of metal-clad buildings, paved parking lots, patches of lawn struggling to grow on the sandy soil, a vast blue sky, and beyond, endless stands of black spruce. I suddenly wonder whether an entire summer here won't prove a bit much. "We'll see," I say to myself. "At least my return ticket is an open one!" I go to pick up my bag at the side of the bus.

"How was the trip?" Chip asks, as he shows me to a green pickup truck.

"Endless," I answer. "I slept a lot. After my exams though, it's good to get away."

"They went well?"

"My exams? Terribly. I'm seriously worried. I may even have flunked Statistics."

Chip tries to reassure me. "Don't worry, David. It's always like that with exams. I'm sure that when your marks come, you'll be delighted."

We drive past a hospital, a handsome low, spread-out building with nice touches of colour to its facade, and then turn into a residential area. We are both feeling a little awkward and there are pauses in our conversation. "Mum sends you her best wishes," I say. On the way, I had stopped with my mother for two days in Baie-Comeau.

"Thanks. How is she?"

"She's very well," I say. "I had a good visit with her." I have difficulty thinking of something else to say. "She teaches French literature at high school and loves it."

What I am really thinking about is the moment when Mum burst into tears and told me how ashamed she had been when she first realised that she was pregnant. "You can't imagine how terrible I felt, David. I knew by then that my marriage was over, that it was a failure. And then, suddenly, I found myself pregnant; I was going to be a mother, but I couldn't admit who was the father."

Chip slows down to let an elderly couple cross the street. "Yes, she has told me about her teaching. She'll be coming to stay with us here as soon as school is out."

"Yes. She told me."

"She is thinking of retiring at the end of this year. That would be great."

I look at Chip with surprise. "Have you seen her since we were together in Baie-Comeau?"

He hesitates and gives a little smile. "Yes. Once."

We turn into a driveway and get out of the truck. "This is it, David. Chateau Forbes. Welcome, and come on in."

His house is set back from the road, with willow and alders separating it from what seems to be the beginnings of the spruce forest which constantly invades the town. Inside, it is sparsely furnished, but comfortable. Chip shows me to a small room at the back. This is to be my home for the summer.

Two months! This is where I stay for the next two months. Living with Chip, whom I hardly know; my uncle who has turned out to be my father. And for a while with my mother, whom I also barely know. "This had better work out well," I say to myself, "otherwise it's going to be a long summer!"

That evening, Chip cooks two steaks on the barbecue in his back yard and I help him. We both start to relax. It is easier for us to do something together than just to talk.

He hands me a glass of wine. "What did you think of the Trans- Labrador Highway?"

"Amazing," I reply. "All those rivers and lakes. It just doesn't stop. It makes you sort of dreamy."

He agrees. "Each time I see one of those lakes I want to take out my canoe and go exploring, cross the lake to look for its source, see what lies beyond the next point. One of my ambitions for this summer is for us to go on a good canoe trip together. Would you like that?"

I am pleased at the idea. "Sounds great. That would be a new experience for sure. Where would we go?"

"One of the rivers up north. I haven't decided yet."

"Just don't make it too difficult. I don't think I have ever been in a canoe. I have zero experience."

Chip laughs. "It's easy. I can show you." He changes the subject. "Tell me about Leo. What did he say when you told him that you were coming up here for the summer?"

"At first, he was angry and said I would be bored stiff. Then he calmed down a bit. These days he is moody and doesn't say very much."

"Does he ever mention Grandad or the fire?"

"Occasionally. He sure doesn't pull his punches when he talks about you."

"Yes," Chip says with a laugh. "I'm not surprised." Chip tells me that he has engaged a lawyer in Montreal to contest Grandad's handwritten will on the grounds that at the time he made it, he was no longer mentally competent. "I have also asked him to check Grandad's finances as well. His bank account and brokerage accounts. Just to make sure that everything is kosher."

"Kosher?" I ask.

"Leo has been running your grandfather's finances for the last ten years or so. I just hope he hasn't been helping himself at the same time."

My heart sinks. At this point I don't want any more complications. "I hope so too."

We finish our steaks and I am beginning to feel like a new man. "Tell me, Chip," I start to ask. "Did you ever realise... did you ever think that Mum's pregnancy..."

He interrupts me, with an embarrassed smile. "Absolutely not, David. Honestly. She and I saw little or nothing of each other after that night. I think we both regretted it and simply wanted to put it behind us. That was certainly my reaction at the time. What your mother told us that day in Baie-Comeau came to me as a complete surprise. I was stunned."

"When did you hear of my birth?" I ask him.

"Only several years later. I think that the first thing I heard was that they had separated and divorced. Then I learned that you had been born and were living with Leo. It never occurred to me that he was not your father. I apologise David, if that's the right thing to do."

We both think about this in silence. "For my part," I finally say, "I don't think you really need to apologise. What happened, happened. It sure makes things complicated though. Do you think Leo suspects anything?"

"No." Chip shakes his head. "I doubt that very much from what you have told me."

I turn my wine glass thoughtfully in my hand and

then, for no particular reason, think of my Inuit carving. "Chip," I say, "I almost forgot. I have something really interesting to show you." I rise and go into the house to fetch the Inuit head.

"This is lovely," he says when I have returned and shown it to him. "Where did you get it?" When I say that it comes from Grandad, he becomes really interested, particularly when I describe the way in which Grandad gave it to me. "What did Grandad have in mind," he muses, "and why keep it secret from Leo?"

"I think that Grandad wanted me to have it for some special reason, and that he was afraid that my father would take it away from me. I also think that Grandad would be happy to know that I am now visiting Labrador. However, the whole thing's a mystery. I like the carving a lot, don't you?"

"Yes, I do. Very much so. I know someone who could give us a good idea of where it comes from. George Walker. He's an archeologist, works out on Huntingdon Island."

I also take out the envelope full of documents that Jane gave me. He gives a little smile as he reads the seven letters from "M".

"Good old Grandad. He seems to have made a conquest there. A schoolteacher in Hopedale, and why not!" He rereads the last letter and frowns a bit. "It's rather strange. They seem to have been close, but at the end something happened and their friendship stopped. No more letters from Mary, or Martha, or Melissa, or whatever her name was."

The light is beginning to fade and the mosquitos have discovered us, so we pick up our plates and glasses and take them back into the kitchen.

As we are washing up, Chip asks me about the Steak House fire. "When you got back to the house from university that evening, was it late?"

"Not very. Perhaps eight or nine o'clock."

"And was Leo there?"

"He says so, but I went straight to my room and didn't see him. He could have been in the kitchen I suppose. I can't be sure."

Chip thinks for a moment. "Was it a clear night, or was it snowing?"

"It was snowing quite hard."

"And were there footprints in the snow in front of the house when you arrived? On the steps going up to the front door?"

"*And were there footprints?*" I think hard. Yes, of course there were. "Yes," I answer. "There was one set of footprints. They looked like Leo's." I force myself to remember. "And they were leading down the steps, away from the house."

Chip nods his head thoughtfully. "David. I think Leo's in it right up to his neck. Just what happens next, we shall see. You go get some sleep. I leave early for work tomorrow, so sleep in as long as you like. There's plenty in the fridge. Just help yourself."

18

The next day, Chip returns from work and tells me that he is planning a trip to Nain. "I have to meet some people in local government up there. At the same time, I'll bring along Dad's ashes and have them buried somewhere near where he used to live. Would you like to join me?"

"Of course, I would," I reply. I have now heard so much about the northern coast of Labrador that I am anxious to see it for myself. We decide that I should leave a day or two before him and take the coastal ferry.

"It's the scenic route." Chip laughs. "As long as the sea is not too rough."

We go down to an office next to the big wharf by a place called Otter Creek, and I make my reservation. The ferry is a trusty old workhorse called the *Northern Ranger*; it carries both passengers and cargo. It will stop at five villages on its way to Nain and take about three days to make the passage.

On the day of my departure, I present myself at the ferry office two hours before the *Ranger* is due to leave. The wharf is busy with trucks and containers, and we passengers wait our turn before making our way through all of the bustle on the wharf to the gangway of the ferry. Soon after, the ship is fully loaded and we cast off and head out down Hamilton Inlet.

I have never travelled on a proper ship before and find it a wonderful experience. You are like a prisoner, confined in a small space and suspended in time. There is nothing to do but wait patiently and let the shoreline gradually reveal itself beyond those endless grey seas. I spend much of my time stretched out in a chair in the lounge reading or looking absent-mindedly out the window.

Periodically, I go on deck to get some air and see what there is to see. For the first part of the voyage, there are endless little islands and bays, low mountains covered with trees, and occasional rafts of black duck and sightings of minke whales. No matter how warmly I'm dressed, I always end up getting a bit cold out there and needing to go back in to warm up.

My fellow passengers are mostly Métis or native, both Inuit and Innu. They sit about in groups surrounded by their bags and their boxes. At mealtimes, a bell sounds and we all take our turn at the cafeteria counter along one side of the lounge. There are also cabins for those who wish, but I have chosen to travel steerage.

Our first stop is Rigolet. While the vessel is unloading and then reloading, I am able to take a quick stroll around the village. It is a primarily Inuit and Métis village of some three hundred people. There is a cluster of larger buildings about the wharf area, and then a long boardwalk that leaves the village and runs along the coast for a considerable distance. The former Hudson's Bay post has been preserved as a museum.

Back on board the *Ranger,* I strike up a conversation with a woman on the afterdeck as we watch Rigolet gradually disappearing from sight. "How is it that there are so many French names up here?" I ask her. During my brief stroll onshore, I had read a plaque stating that Rigolet was established in 1735 as a trading post by a French-Canadian trader named Louis Fornel. I would like to know more.

She smiles and seems pleased to share a conversation. Her features suggest that she is partly Inuit. "French and Basque fishermen and whalers came here a lot in the early days. It started in the sixteenth century if not before."

"At one point in time," I say, "that must have changed." I'm thinking of all the signs of a later English influence.

"Yes," she explains. "Things changed in 1763 at the end of the Seven Years War when Labrador was ceded to England. From then on, the French presence up here gradually declined and that of the English became dominant."

I am still thinking of the French names that I have seen on the map. "But the names remain," I say. "Like Groswater Bay and Double Mer."

My companion laughs. "First names too. Mine is Francine, and I have a cousin called Claudette." We chat on, and I learn that she lives and teaches in Hopedale.

After Rigolet, there is a long passage eastwards out to the broad Atlantic, and then the *Ranger* turns north. The swell picks up and the seas are a steely grey, speckled white with spindrift and spume. The coast is one long rugged vista of primeval rock worn smooth and bare by wind, ice and rain. There are few trees to be seen. The sight is at once forbidding and beautiful.

We pass endless islets, flashing white where the waves break over their rocks. We see several icebergs making their slow progress down the coast. Time goes by, and I am constantly falling asleep over my book. It is forced idleness and I enjoy every minute of it.

I am awakened by a jolt and a thud. We are docking at our second stop, Makkovik. A number of disembarking passengers are lined up at the top of the stairs leading down to where the gangway will permit them to disembark. I close my book and look at them, bags in hand, pushing and shoving, eager to be back home.

Emerging in the corridor leading from the cabins are two women: a mother and her daughter it seems to me. Both are carrying a small bag. The girl is very attractive. She is slim, with long black hair tied up in a ponytail under a navy-blue baseball hat. She must be my age, or a bit younger. They are talking quietly together and although I can't be sure, it seems to me that they are speaking Inuktitut. The girl is smiling as she talks to her mother. Perhaps they are sharing some pleasant memory, perhaps a joke. There is something familiar about her, but I'm not sure why.

I go out on deck to look at the town. Our stop is short, and continuing passengers have been asked to stay on board while the cargo is dealt with. Below me, groups of villagers are standing about on the dock, waiting for their parcels, friends, and family.

Now I see our passengers arriving on the wharf, carefully making their way between the forklifts and containers, the pickup trucks and the quad bikes.

After a while the mother and her daughter appear. A sizeable welcoming committee seems to be waiting for them. An elderly woman steps forward, clearly the matriarch, as the others all wait respectfully. She embraces the two, first the mother and then the girl.

It is at that moment that I realise with astonishment why the girl seems so familiar to me. She is the girl whom I saw with her grandmother two or three years previously in Montreal, at the residence for homeless persons. She is the girl of the Inuit head. I have found the girl of my dreams!

She has now finished with family greetings and joined three other girls of her own age who have been standing to one side. There are lots of kisses and hugs, laughs and smiles. The four join arms and leave the wharf area. The girl with the baseball hat is the tallest of the four. She is clearly their leader, the one that the others look up to.

Once more Francine, the teacher from Hopedale, is close by, leaning on the rail. We are both enjoying the same scene. "She's very talented, that one." She points at the girl with the baseball hat. "She writes beautiful poetry."

"What is her name?" I ask.

"Akna. Her name is Akna."

19

The rest of the trip is very scenic. We enjoy generally sunny weather, the broad blue sky dotted with puffy cumulus clouds that a brisk westerly wind is sending straight across to Greenland. The boat stops briefly at Postville, Hopedale, Natuashish, and finally heads for Nain. I spend almost all my time on deck taking in the new sights and thinking of the girl called Akna.

The approach to Nain, the last thirty kilometres or so, is spectacular. We thread our way between numerous rocky islands, and gradually the landscape becomes less severe and more welcoming. Nain itself looks very much like the other coastal villages, only somewhat bigger. It also looks more nordic, and the population, decidedly more Inuit.

Chip has already arrived and finished with his government business. Together, we sit down for supper at the hotel. "I lived up here in the early 80s," he recalls. "It sure has changed since then. I guess the mine at Voisey Bay has had a big impact."

"When did Grandad stop living up here?" I ask.

"About 1998," Chip guesses. "No, it must have been later. About 2000. He had a house near the Moravian church, where we are going to take his ashes tomorrow."

"His last letter to M was in 1987," I say. We both fall silent, wondering what the relationship between Grandad and M might have been and why it was so suddenly terminated.

Back in our room I have difficulty falling asleep. I just can't stop thinking of Akna. "Chip." I say "On the ferry there was a girl whom I once met in Montreal. She left the boat at Makkovik."

"Tell me some other time," Chip answers sleepily. "It's getting late."

The next morning is cold and the wind is from the east. There is a bit of wet in the air. We head over to the Moravian church. A neat white sign proclaims the Moravian motto.

> *"In essentials, unity.*
> *In non-essentials, liberty.*
> *In all things, love."*

The Minister is already there by the church, waiting for us and chatting with three others, two men and an elderly woman. They are visibly local, and I think that they must have known Grandad. Chip goes up to them and hands the Minister a little mahogany box with Grandad's ashes.

We gather together in a circle and the Minister says a few kind words. He is an older man and remembers Grandad. Chip adds his own thoughts and his last words seem apt. "From nothing we come, and to nothing we return." I think Grandad would have liked that.

My own memories of Grandad come flooding back, and for a while I have to fight back the tears. At least this windswept hillside is where he would have wished to come to rest.

The elderly woman comes up to us afterwards. She is wearing a red wind jacket and a green headscarf. She is stocky and of medium height and has a broad, intelligent face. "He was a good man. Up here, we called him 'the Eagle'. Thank you for bringing his ashes back to Nain."

I remember the words in one of the letters: "You are my eagle."

I look at Chip and our eyes meet. "I am his younger son," he says to her. "My name is Chip Forbes. And this is his grandson, David." He waits, but she chooses not to give her own name.

"Didn't you once teach in Hopedale?" he asks her. She nods silently. "And you and he were good friends, I think," Chip continues. Again, she merely nods and turns to go.

"And then what happened?" Chip insists. "What happened to end your friendship?"

She shakes her head. "We remained friends. It's just we stopped seeing each other."

She walks off with a slow dignity, and we ourselves thank the Minister and make our way down to the dock, where it is time for me to say goodbye to Chip and go on board the *Ranger*.

I reclaim my favourite seat in the lounge as we pull out of the harbour and head back south. A fresh offshore breeze is blowing as we thread our way amongst the islands and headlands. I start to think about all the new elements that have recently come into my life, Chip, my mother, Labrador and perhaps even the girl called Akna.

Labrador! This land is beginning to hold me under its spell. Looking out over the water, I have a wonderful feeling of peace and freedom. This is not something I have felt before, certainly not in Montreal. I am rapidly falling in love with this land of sea and rock, river and forest. I find the faces of its inhabitants of endless interest. Its vast spaces make me dream and feel happy.

At each stop, I am able to get off the ferry and take a quick turn around the village. When we reach Makkovik the following morning, I go ashore for a quick stroll while the ship takes on cargo.

Makkovik has a population of about three hundred and the houses, which for the most part are of recent construction and look very comfortable, are either spread out along the water's edge or along a steep road which heads up the hill. You are constantly aware of the ocean, as the village lies along the side of an inlet, which is either open water or the beginnings of a rocky mud flat depending on the state of the tide.

I choose a steep road leading up from the harbour area, and in ten minutes or so reach a modern school building and beside it what looks like a hockey arena. The village stops here; beyond is an endless natural vista of rolling hills and mosses.

There are a number of students coming and going and I scan their faces in the hope of seeing Akna. My imagination begins to run away with itself. I think up a conversation between Akna and me in which I explain that I once saw her in Montreal and then again on the ferry coming north. The conversation leads nowhere so I give up and start again. I imagine myself asking her if the school is good and if the big building beside it is a hockey arena. This sounds no better and I try to stop thinking about her, but without success.

There are fewer students now, and certainly none looking like they might be Akna, so I turn back down the hill. The ferry leaves in half-an-hour. I can see it below, looking enormous in comparison with everything else in the inlet. A pickup truck comes up the hill and passes me, and then a quad bike. Off to my right a man is unloading firewood from a trailer. I pass a handicraft store and turn towards the wharf.

I can hear another quad bike coming fast down the hill behind me, and am forced to move over to the side of the road. Looking back over my shoulder my heart skips a beat: there she is, Akna! She shoots by me wearing a big smile and waving with one hand. I start to wave back.

Then I hear a girl's voice behind me. "Hi ya, Akna!" Akna's eyes were looking straight past me. "Hi ya, Millie," she shouts as she disappears in a cloud of dust.

20

The following weekend, Chip and I set out for the village of Cartwright on the Atlantic coast east of Goose Bay, a drive of about four hundred kilometres. It will take us close to six hours. The weather is bright and sunny - perfect summer weather. Our plan is to meet up with Chip's archeologist friend, George Walker, and show him my Inuit sculpture. In addition, we are to be treated to a trip out to Huntingdon Island to see what George and his team have unearthed there.

"It's incredible, David, the resilience of the people who have been living along this coast over the years." Chip is giving me a primer on the history of Labrador. "For example, although there are plenty of trees around us here," he points out the window of the truck, "when you get to the coast itself, the headlands and the islands, everything is rocky and bare. To live out there, the people made themselves sod houses, sometimes quite big inside, but in sod all the same. There was little wood to speak of, so they built in sod. My friend George has been excavating some of them."

"Why live there at all?" I ask.

"For the Inuit, it was familiar. They originally came from further up the coast, north of the tree line. On the other hand, for the families of mixed Inuit and European blood, the Métis, it was to fish for cod and hunt seal. They were out on the coast mainly in the summertime. In the winter, they would move inland to where there was hunting and firewood."

"Do people object to being referred to as Métis?" I ask. "Does it risk upsetting them?"

"No more. They're now quite proud of it, and rightly so."

After an hour or two, we change places and he lets me drive. At one point, I have to slow down while a mother bear crosses the road with her two cubs. They are very visible, as there is nothing else in the landscape that is so black.

"Don't expect too much of Cartwright," Chip says. "Its population is only four or five hundred. The ferry stops there and there is a fish-freezing plant. That's about all. However, the location is very pretty."

When we arrive, George is there at the hotel to greet us. He is about ten years older than me, short and stocky, very serious, and with a mess of curly red hair. The three of us sit down for a bite of supper.

"Show George your Inuit head, David," suggests Chip. I produce it out of my pocket and George examines it carefully. "An amulet," he says thoughtfully. "I'm no geologist, but I would say that it's too dark to be soapstone. It is more likely serpentine. The face is interesting."

He turns it over in his hand. "The work is certainly of a high quality." I point out the hole through the back and George explains that the head would have been attached by a leather thong to someone's clothing, possibly as an amulet to ward off evil spirits. He notices a seal scratched on the base of the carving and we speculate on its significance.

"It reminds me of something I've seen before," George reflects. "The oval face, the wide chin. There was a man up near Hopedale who did work like that. I'll try to remember his name. It's a fine piece. It seems to exert a special force."

I laugh. "As long as it wards off the evil spirits I'll be happy."

The next morning, George comes to meet us and takes us down to the little harbour. There is a wharf for fishing boats, but he is tied up to a wooden structure nearby. We put on our life jackets. "Good weather. Should be a nice trip."

Huntingdon Island turns out to be very interesting. The archeologists have set up a couple of tents near where they are working. The landscape is windswept and hostile. We beach our boat beside two others and walk across the rocks to the place where George's team is at work. What we see onsite are several groups of floor stones set in a particular round pattern, each group indicating the location of an original sod house, probably dating as far back as the mid-eighteenth century.

"There was a sort of tunnel leading into each house," George explains, "and each tunnel had a dip in the passageway that served as a cold trap. Inside there was a common space in the middle and raised sleeping berths along the sides made of sand and gravel. The berths would have been covered with branches and hides."

"What did a house actually look like from the outside?" I ask.

"It was bulky and sort of igloo shaped. They built them half sunk into the ground so as to be able to capture the heat rising from below. They rarely lived in the same house for more than a season or two, so the houses rapidly returned to nature."

"Could you stand up inside?" asks Chip.

George looks at the two of us. "'Not if you're tall like you are," he says with a grin.

"Have you found many objects or artefacts?" Chip enquires.

"Yes," says George. "Mostly, the standard European goods such as nails, fishhooks, and the like. Also some Inuit ones, such as oil lamps and ulus." We walk over to where a girl is crouched down on a bare rock, carefully cleaning something. "There you go," George says. "That's an ulu that Jill has found." I can see that it is a curved blade of stone some four inches across. "It was used as a knife," explains George, "to skin animals, cut them up and scrape the hides."

After a short visit, George takes us back to Cartwright. "I thought a bit more about your amulet," he says to me as we part company in front of the hotel, "and I spoke to a friend from Hopedale. There was a man who worked on the fishing boats and who came from Postville. Everyone called him BG. Those were his initials, I guess. On his trips, he would carve small stones just to pass the time. His carvings became well known and he signed them on the bottom with a seal. Let's have another look at yours."

We have another look at the carving, and George points out the seal on the underside. "People used to wear them on their clothes on special occasions," he says. "Particularly the young girls."

Chip and I thank George and start our long journey back to Goose Bay. I take the wheel for the first two hours. "The stream we're crossing just now flows into the Eagle River," Chip explains at one point. "The road here makes a long loop to the south so as to avoid the Eagle River watershed." I nod, concentrating on the road ahead. It is straight and wide and there is absolutely no traffic.

"The Eagle is a wonderful river," he adds. "I canoed it last summer with a friend. We were taken in by float plane to a place called Camp 1155."

"Why Camp 1155? Are there as many camps as all that?"

He laughs. "No, it's called that because it's at 1155 feet above sea level. About three-hundred and sixty metres. From there to salt water it's about one-hundred and eighty kilometres, so on average we were descending about two metres per kilometre, a good average for canoeing a Labrador river. In any event, you certainly don't want it much steeper than that."

"Was it easy?" I ask.

"No! It was damn hard. There is a stretch in the middle called the Gorge, about seven kilometres in length. It took us an entire day. We were constantly paddling short stretches, then getting out and carrying everything up the bank and around a cliff, then lowering the loaded canoe by rope down a bit of rapid, then paddling yet another short stretch. At one point, there is a bit of calmer water and we crossed from one bank to the other."

"In the middle of the afternoon, we came to a place called the Devil's Gap, where the entire Eagle River squeezes through a narrow opening between two cliffs. What a sight! Fortunately, at this point we were on the right side of the river, found a trail, and with another hour's hard work, carried everything down to the quiet water below."

I suggest that when we do our canoe trip together, Chip find us an easier river! He smiles. "I have already chosen it. Be prepared!"

It is dark when we get back to Goose Bay. As we arrive

Chip turns to me. "You would never guess it would you, but George's grandmother was half Inuit. It's always like that up here."

21

Two days later, we are both at the airport to welcome Mum. It is a gorgeous summer day and Goose Bay is looking its best.

I examine Chip. He seems excited. He has put on a clean shirt, and I heard him whistling a little tune this morning as he cleaned the kitchen. It sets me wondering.

I'm excited as well. Mum and I have met several times now and I have also talked to her on the telephone. Less and less do I think of all those years without her. More and more, it is somehow as though she had always been there.

She gets off the plane and we can see her from a distance, her head bowed as she reaches deep into her purse for some sunglasses.

Back at Chip's house, there is an amusing moment when Chip shows her to the guest bedroom. "Unless you prefer..." he starts to say with a big smile. "No," she says sternly, taking possession of her room. "This will be fine."

Chip and I have prepared fish for dinner with a decent bottle of white wine, and over the table Mum tells us a bit about the years she once spent in Goose Bay. "There wasn't an awful lot to do. I made one or two friends and we used to meet for tea and go for long walks together. In winter, I also skied a lot, downhill and cross-country."

"Did you travel up the Labrador coast?" I ask. "Or visit Grandad in Nain?"

"No. Leo never took me on his trips, and he wasn't too happy with the idea that I should go off on my own. Grandad sometimes came down from Nain to visit us."

"We met a former friend of his in Nain," Chip says. "Taught school in Hopedale. She was there at the church when we met the minister and gave him Grandad's ashes. David, why don't you go get the letters to show your mum?"

I do so and Mum reads them carefully. "She has a very neat hand," she says. "She must have been a good teacher! Grandad never mentioned her. Still, it's nice to think that he wasn't always alone."

"Yes," agrees Chip. "It is sad living alone."

"Are you sad?" Mum teases him. "You don't look it." Chip grins.

We finish our dinner and start to clear the table. Mum fills the sink with hot water and adds the detergent. "Here, David. You wash. Pass me that towel, I can dry!" Chip leaves us to make a phone call.

"How are you getting on with your new father?" Mum asks me when the two of us are alone.

I consider my reply with care. "We're getting on well, Mum. Honestly. He's not being pushy, and gradually, we are getting there. I think it's going to be just fine."

"He's a good man," she says. "*Mon Dieu.* The two brothers are so different!"

"In what way?" I ask with interest. "How would you put it?"

It is her turn to consider her reply. "Basically, Leo thinks of himself first, whilst Chip thinks of others." I nod my agreement.

"Tell me, Val," asks Chip who has just reappeared. "Why do you think Leo wanted to leave Goose Bay?" He puts a special emphasis on the "you". "And why on such short notice? Was his business in trouble in some way?"

"Leo never told me anything about his business. I think that his decision was taken because of something else. Possibly connected with the business. I never did figure it out."

"Was it something that you wanted?" I ask. "Did he do so for your sake?"

Mum laughs bitterly. "Dream on, David. Dream on!"

We tell Mum about our recent trip to Cartwright and she scolds us. "Why didn't you wait? I would have liked to go too."

"Another time, Val," Chip says. "It's because David has a little Inuit carving and we wanted to ask the archeologist doing the dig on Huntingdon Island if he recognised it in any way."

"I haven't shown it to you yet, Mum," I say. "Grandad gave it to me. Would you like to see it?"

"Of course," she replies. "Let's have a look." I go to my room to fetch it and hand it to her.

She looks at us both, one after the other, and starts to laugh. "He got it from me." She can see the surprise written on both our faces, and just in order to tease us a bit takes her time and pretends to be searching back in her memory.

"When we were just married and still living here in Goose Bay, Leo was often up north on business. He began to go off for longer and longer periods, and I began to fear that he was cheating on me. The signs were there."

She pauses. "One time, Leo came back, I think it was from Hopedale, and he was acting in a strange way. He complained that he wasn't feeling well and went to take a shower. I was tidying up his clothes when I found a little carving in his pocket. This one." She holds up my amulet for inspection. "I remember the general shape, the wide chin, the hole at the back. Yes! This is the one that I found in his pocket."

Chip is looking at her in a curious way. "So, you kept it?"

"Well, yes," Mum continues. "I imagined that the woman he was seeing had given it to him. I thought that by hiding it, I would somehow send him a signal to stop seeing her, to behave himself."

"And then?"

"It was right afterwards that Leo decided that he no longer wanted to live in Goose Bay and that we should move to Montreal."

"How did Grandad get the amulet then?" I ask.

"When he learned that we were about to leave, he came down from Nain to say goodbye. While Leo was out of the house, I fetched the amulet and showed it to Grandad. He said he would keep it safe for me, and I was more than happy to accept. Once I had taken it, I didn't want Leo to know. He would have beaten the living daylights out of me. He had already done so before for less than that."

"Grandad didn't want me to show it to Dad!" I exclaim. "Grandad was very clear about it. He must have been afraid that Dad would take it away from me."

Mum is following all this with interest. "Why would Leo have done so?" she muses. "What was it doing in his pocket in the first place, and why would he subsequently wish to have it back?"

"And why would Grandad not wish him to take it back?" Chip adds. He picks the carving up from the table where Mum has left it and looks at it closely. "If only stones could talk."

Our summer together passes by all too quickly. I receive my marks from university, and they are not so bad after all. Chip and I go for a jog most mornings; there is a good path that runs through the trees near the back of his house and we take it down to the commercial part of Goose Bay, then up to the area near the airport, and then back home again. It takes us about half an hour.

I make a new friend thanks to Chip, who knows his father. The friend's name is Andrew and he is an Innu from Sheshatshiu, a village about thirty kilometres north of Goose Bay. Andrew is my age, heavily built and has long black hair that he ties up in a knot. He has a canoe with a small motor at the back and often takes me fishing for trout on Grand Lake, a long lake lying behind Sheshatshiu.

I ask him about the band council at Sheshatshiu. Andrew tells me that there is a chief and six councillors, his father being one. They meet regularly, their main responsibilities being health, education and social welfare. He is proud of his dad and also of being Innu. "We were living here several thousand years ago," he tells me. "Before both the Inuit and the white men came to this country."

Over the summer, I can see a new relationship emerging between Chip and my mother. They go for long walks together, she grasping him by the arm. Increasingly they look like a couple, and I suppose increasingly the three of us look like a family, which in fact we are.

At the end of August, Mum takes leave of us, with multiple hugs and kisses, in order to return to Baie-Comeau. "My last year," she announces. "This will be my last year teaching. After that I retire and who knows?"

Chip and I now start preparations for our canoe trip, which will take us down a river called the Kanairiktok.

We're off! The Twin Otter is climbing to one thousand metres, crammed with the two of us, Chip's canoe and two big waterproof packsacks. Looking out the window, I can see Grand Lake below us and recognise some of the spots where I have been fishing with Andrew.

Our pilot is called Jack. He is a friend of Chip and is doing us a favour. He has a group of prospectors to fetch back to Goose Bay and rather than flying north empty, he is giving us a lift. It is the start of September, and the bugs shouldn't be too bad. If all goes well, our trip will take us about a week.

After a little over one hour, Jack circles low over Shipiskan Lake, checking for logs and other perils, and then sets us down near the discharge. Out goes the canoe. Then it's our turn, with our two packs and assorted gear, and off flies Jack, leaving us feeling very lonely: two small mortals in an enormous, seemingly infinite landscape. We head for a nearby sandy beach where we will spend the first night.

It happens to be a strange spot. The Innu come here

a lot to hunt in the fall and winter, and make camp at the very spot which we have chosen. Scattered about are various signs of their presence, including an assortment of discarded ski-doo parts. There is the odd grave, marked by a white cross. Most remarkably, there is a glass cabinet, standing under a big spruce tree, with statuettes of the Virgin Mary and Joseph inside, together with sundry mementoes such as plastic dolls and spent shotgun shells.

We immediately start setting up camp. We cut five saplings and bind them together to make a frame for the tent. Our tent is a typical Labrador trapper's tent, about two metres square, in canvas that once was white, with a light fly over the top. It has no floor of its own. This we make with fir boughs, and the smell inside is delicious. We have with us a tin stove the size of a shoe box, and we set it up on flat stones inside the tent and install a little tin chimney which exits the wall of the tent through a hole made in a special non-flammable material. We have a quick supper of ham and eggs and turn in.

Next morning, I raise the wall of the tent beside my head and look outside. The morning is misty and cold and the tip of my nose is numb. Chip lights a fire in the stove, it crackles and roars, and after a short while I am so cosy in my sleeping bag that I could stay there all day. After toast and tea, we break camp and load our canoe. My boots are thigh waders and feel cold when I pull them on.

It is a good canoe, almost five metres long and slightly more than twenty kilos in weight. When we travel in it, we tie everything carefully down at the thwarts. There is a third paddle in case of breaks. We have an axe, but decided we could fend off any bears without the help of a rifle. Chip takes the stern and I the bow.

Running the discharge from the lake is fast, but easy. The bottom is sandy, there are no boulders. Along the shore, we notice wolf and bear sign. We also see a bald eagle overhead.

We soon reach a junction with the main branch of the river. There is a lot of flow coming in from our right. At this point, the river is some seventy-five metres wide. We turn upstream, just to explore, and struggle all day against a powerful current to reach a point about fourteen kilometres above the junction. Sometimes we paddle, but often we take turns pulling the canoe with its bow rope, splashing along in the shallows. At the end of our day, we camp for a second night. We are about one-hundred and fifty metres above sea level, and two hundred kilometres from the estuary of the river.

The view from our tent is south across the river. In the distance is a large table-topped mountain. Nearer to hand, the river is fringed with poplar, giving a nice grey shade to set off the dark greens of the black spruce and balsam fir. Just upstream are rapids and I fall asleep listening to the water as it chatters and chuckles outside.

The next morning, we turn about and head downstream. The swift current bears us effortlessly along. I am beginning to understand my role in the bow: to spot underwater rocks, make minor changes to our direction, and hold the canoe straight against sudden gusts of wind. At one point, we come to some islands and at the tip of one stands a big bull moose. On our approach, his enormous ears go straight up and he trots away across the top of a beaver lodge. On a beach we see his hoof prints. They are a good ten inches across.

We will have travelled about fifty kilometres today, amazing, but it is all swift. That night, a lone wolf serenades us from across the river. After a short while, a few more wolves join in.

The third day, we continue downstream. The river

flows through a deep valley. There are numerous streams feeding into it, and as we tend to stay close to one shore or the other, we are able to notice animal tracks in the sand and mud along the edge of the river. At one feeder we see a strange sight: a porcupine swimming awkwardly across from one side of the little stream to the other. "It's floating very high in the water," I observe. "That's funny."

"It's because its quills are hollow," Chip explains.

As we continue along, I am struck by a series of thoughts. Firstly, how lucky I am just to be here with Chip. (Very lucky!) Next, how many people have seen a porcupine swim? (Very few.) Finally, I think of Akna and wish that she was here with me so we could have seen that porcupine together.

There is a thud; our canoe has struck an underwater rock. "David," calls out Chip from the stern. "Wake up!"

So far, there have been no serious rapids and the river starts to meander through numerous sandbanks. Towards the end of our day, we approach a large lake named Snegamook and make camp. It is worth mentioning the delicious dinner that we make for ourselves: fried chunks of bacon, dried tomatoes and tagliatelle. Fit for a king!

I have started calling Chip "Dad". It started more or less by accident. I was back in the bush fetching wood for the fire and for a moment couldn't see where I was. "Dad!" I shouted out. "Dad! Where are you?"

"Over here, over here," came the answer.

When I arrived back at the tent, my arms full of dry spruce branches, he said, "David, you just called me 'Dad'. I hope you'll continue to do so." I could tell that he was very happy.

More and more it is how I view him: my father. We have really good conversations, as we lie in the tent on each side of the stove. He tells me about his early life and quizzes me about mine. "Leo and I were quite close at one point in time," he says. "Perhaps that was thanks to Mum. After she died though, we went our separate ways, Leo to Montreal and I to Nain. My years in Nain with your grandad were wonderful. We went fishing for char in the Fraser Canyon and backpacked up in the Torngats. Heavens above, David! You should see the Torngats."

"You're really fond of nature, aren't you?"

"I guess so. You know, David, the future of mankind lies with nature, or not at all."

"What do you mean?"

"Simply that. We have no future on this planet unless we save it. For that we must stop pursuing individual goals and set ourselves collective ones. If we don't, we will have wasted all this beauty." He waves vaguely towards the outside of the tent.

"You make it sound like a religion."

"In a sense it is a religion. Christianity and the other religions used to act to curb our excesses. With some success, I suppose. However, they offer little to help us when it comes to curbing our present, excessive individualism. It is that which is leading to the destruction of our planet, and we can't even see it."

I tell him that I have difficulties with religion. We end up agreeing that religion and ideology should not prevent people from behaving rationally and exercising their critical judgement.

On the next day, the lake broadens and we paddle along its northern shore. High up on a bank, we see something white and go to investigate. It is a grave, and on a marble cross we can read the following.

TSHINISH CHIEF DIED NOV. 12 1926 AET 80 YRS

His people must have had a high regard for him, erecting this memorial to him in this special place. One day, I must find out more about Tshinish.

Most of the day, we spend on Lake Snegamook. Paddling a distance on a lake can be a bit monotonous; the vistas are vast and it seems to take an age just to reach the next point or to cross the next bay. I find myself repeating in my head a tune that happens to coincide with the rhythm at which we paddle, my favourite being a melody from a symphony by Sibelius.

On a large lake in a river system, it is not always easy to find the outlet. There is the risk of entering bay after bay, only to be disappointed. One indicator is to detect the current by looking at the seaweeds growing on the bottom of the lake. As long as they are not affected by the wind, they will point the way the current is flowing. On Snegamook, we finally enter a shallow sandy area where the weeds tell us to continue to the bottom of the adjoining bay. Here, to our joy, we find the discharge of the lake and rejoin the Kanairiktok River.

We cross a succession of small lakes and at one point the river deepens and narrows and forms two massive eddies, one on each side. In the middle of each eddy is a vortex which we carefully stay clear of. Ahead of us we are beginning to hear the river.

Dad is now getting cautious, hugging the bank. The noise of the river increases and finally ahead of us we can see a sudden break in our view: in the foreground, flat water, and beyond, treetops. We go ashore at a smooth rock on our left. The sight ahead is spectacular. The river makes an immediate drop of four or five metres in two great spouts, separated by a massive jumble of boulders stranded in the middle of the river. One spout is about twenty-five metres across, the other, somewhat less.

We camp on a sandy beach below the falls on the south side. I throw a line into the water with a fly called a *black bear, green butt.* Thanks to those outings with Andrew on Grand Lake, my casting is improving. In no time flat, I hook a fat *ouananiche,* or landlocked salmon. It will be our dinner.

That night in the tent, we study the map. So far, we have covered about ninety-five kilometres; ahead of us remain about one hundred and ten. At about ten o'clock the northern lights dance for us. It is a beautiful sight.

The trip from here on is a constant challenge. We come to numerous rapids, with Dad standing quickly up in the stern each time to choose the best way down. I ply my paddle, first on one side and then on the other, keeping us from smashing into the rocks. In the rougher parts, we get out of the canoe and splashing down the side of the river, lower the loaded canoe downstream with the ropes. From time to time we reach falls and are obliged to empty the canoe and make a carry over the rocks or into the bush. Needless to say, there are no portage trails. It makes for hard work, but in a typical day we can cover about thirty kilometres.

Dad and I are now a team. We are as one man as we set up camp, cook dinner, load the canoe the next morning, and travel down the Kanairiktok through rain and shine, in flat water and down rapids.

"David," he says to me one lunchtime as we are sitting on a smooth rock beside the river having a boil-up. "How are you coping with the idea that I am your father?" I know what he's thinking. He wants to know if I now feel closer to him than to Leo.

"I don't hold it against you," I answer. "Nor against Mum. But it's not obvious. For example, if I really loved Leo, I imagine I would be very upset."

"Perhaps one way to think about it is to say that if Leo had been a good husband, it wouldn't have happened. If their marriage had been a success, your mother and I wouldn't have done what we did."

"I guess that's right. I'm also not sure how the fact that you are my uncle changes things. It seems to make it easier, but I can't think why."

"Same genes I suppose," he smiles, "and same Grandad."

"You know, Dad. I think you're right. If you had been a stranger, I would have lost my Grandad and that, I would never have forgiven you!" We both smile at the idea.

We get back on our feet, rinse out our mugs and set out once more down the river.

I have learned the all-important technique of eddying-out. When we wish to leave the river and are in fast water or rapids, Dad brings us close to one bank and picks a spot where there is a little eddy that can help us. Then he shouts "eddy out", and I dig hard sideways with my paddle on the same side as the bank, while he drives us forward on the other side. The canoe spins about and we can then reach the bank itself heading upstream. This permits Dad to hold us to shore while I jump out with the rope in my hand.

One day, we start down a long rapid and come to a cliff that sticks out into the river on the side that we are close to. After the cliff, the river disappears in a sharp bend. Not knowing what to expect we are obliged to beach the canoe and go have a look. There are big rapids ahead, so either we go back upstream about a kilometre to where we can safely cross the river to the further bank, which looks easier, or we do a carry over the cliff. We choose the latter.

Carrying the bags across the face of the cliff proves

to be easy enough, but with the canoe it's another matter. We each take an end and start out cautiously across the cliff face. Dad succeeds in making it, but I fall. There is a moment of suspense while he holds on to the canoe by one end, its other end dangling over the edge, and I regain my balance one metre below on a ledge. In the end, we make it and stand there catching our breath on a little beach beyond. I suddenly think of the amulet which is in my pocket.

"Phew!" I say, as I feel it through my rain gear. "It's still there."

"The amulet?"

"Yes. I always keep it on me."

"Your good luck token," Dad says with a smile. "Perhaps it saved you from sliding into the river."

I laugh. "I think it was the ledge that saved me, not the amulet."

That same evening, we discuss women. "Have you a girlfriend these days?" Dad asks me.

"Not right now. I used to have one in Montreal called Irene. Now we've split, although we're still good friends. There is a girl in Makkovik called Akna. We have never properly met, but I'm hoping we will someday." I am flustered. This sounds ridiculous. "What about you, Dad?"

He seems equally embarrassed. "Well...It's not really the same. Your mother, though. That could just turn into something!"

"Tell me, Dad," I say, changing the subject. "Is it true that you left university after your second year?" It is something I have been meaning to ask him for a while. Somehow, it troubles me.

"Yes, David. It's true. I was in economics and found that it didn't really suit me. I was also a bit mixed up at the time. I suppose I was immature. I should have stuck it out, but I didn't." He pauses. "I will say this in my defence, however. The way they taught it, the whole discipline seemed to be aimed at promoting economic growth. Increasingly, I was becoming convinced that economic growth was more something to be avoided than something to be promoted."

One morning, I wake up slowly, stiff from the previous day's efforts and enjoying the warmth of my sleeping bag and the smell of the fire that Dad has lit in the little stove next to my head. "What's that you're doing?" I ask sleepily.

"Making stove bread," comes the answer. "Here, flatten this out and stick it on the side of the stove." I reach a hand out of my sleeping bag and he hands me a little ball of dough.

"What's it made of?"

"Flour and water. With a bit of baking powder and salt. Keep your eye on it. It will fall off when that side is cooked. Then you stick it back on the other side."

Ten minutes later we are eating our hot bread, sliced through the middle and dripping with butter and honey. It is delicious.

The high point of our trip comes a couple of days later when we reach the great falls. First, there is a lesser set of falls, necessitating a lengthy carry over the rocks. The drop here is about five or ten metres.

The river then widens before narrowing again to only thirty metres or so. We stand in awe on the bare rock to one side and look at the entire river as it forms two massive standing waves on the edge of a drop, with white froth boiling two metres into the air. Looking out into the mist and deafened by the sound of the river, we see the entire Kanairiktok fall twenty-five or thirty metres in a sheer sheet of water into the rock-walled, turbulent basin below.

On the rock where we stand is a long log. Others have

carved their initials into it, and we follow suit. Then we carry canoe and bags down the smooth rocks to the water's edge below, load up, and make our way out towards the estuary. This night is to be our last on the river.

"David," says Dad to me as we are setting up the tent. "I can't begin to tell you how much this trip has meant to me, and how happy and proud I am to have you as my son." His face shows great emotion as he speaks.

"Dad," I answer. "It's the same for me." We give each other a big, long, happy hug.

"Next winter, David," Dad says enthusiastically, "I have a plan! We'll take a ski-doo trip together. All the way up the Labrador coast, from Goose Bay to Nain."

I pretend to groan. "Let's get out of here first!"

The next day a friend of Dad's from Hopedale comes with his boat to fetch us as we paddle out into the estuary, father and son, filled with pride at our successful trip down the Kanairiktok.

23

Now I am back in Montreal starting my last year in biology. I love the courses and know that I am on the right path, that with medicine I have made the right choice.

My summer in Goose Bay has left me a different person. I feel much more healthy and self-confident than I was two months ago. The shirts that I left behind are now tight around the collar, and my packsack full of books seems ridiculously light.

Montreal astonishes me after the peace and quiet of Labrador. There are so many people, all seemingly in a rush to go here and there. I can't get over the height of the buildings, the rumour of the traffic. It is all very exciting, but at the same time I miss Labrador.

I have moved into a small apartment on the Plateau with two other students. Dad occasionally sends me money from Goose Bay, but I get by pretty well with a combination of bursaries and student loans. We have some great parties in the apartment. Greg often joins us as well. He has a new girlfriend called Vreni. They have become inseparable. Vreni has heavy, wiry hair gathered in a fierce tangle that falls halfway down her back. It is the colour of red rust. Her eyebrows are thick and bushy, and she is full of fun. She has an incredible collection of necklaces and bracelets which she wears in various impossible combinations.

The Plateau is a fun area to live in. True, it is a bit run down in places, but there is a buzz about it that you can't really find in Saint-Henri and Griffintown.

Occasionally, I go back to see Elka. She tells me that Leo speaks to her occasionally, asking for my news. She feels sorry for him. "You should go see him sometime. The poor old man! He's feeling a bit sorry for himself."

It is a glorious Saturday afternoon in early October when I do so. The trees are beginning to wear their autumn colours, a mixture of bright golds and deep reds, and the leaves make little piles in the corners where they have fallen and the wind has collected them together.

I go up to Leo's front door and ring the bell. I am nervous and feel a little guilty at not having visited him before. He opens the door wearing a dressing gown with shirt and trousers underneath. "Hello, David," he says in a flat, unwelcoming voice. If he is surprised, he doesn't want it to show. "Where have you been?"

"Hello, Dad," I reply with a show of warmth. "You're looking great! How's it going?"

"Come in. Come in." He shuts the door behind us and ushers me into the living room. We sit down facing each other. "How come I haven't seen you for so long? Where have you been?"

"I just got back from Goose Bay."

"Surely," he complains, "you haven't been all that time in Goose Bay? All summer long? Doing what?"

I laugh, perhaps a little cheekily. "It's not so bad. I stayed with Chip. We did all sorts of things together."

"Chip is a damn fool."

"No, he isn't."

"That's no way to talk to your father."

"Look, Dad," I say. "I was just telling you where I've been. If you would prefer that I leave you alone..."

He looks startled and says, "No, no. Wait a minute. You've become awfully sensitive. What's got into you?"

I make a show of sitting down slowly. "What about you? How have you been?"

"I get by. The Steak House is still closed. I haven't touched any money yet from the insurers." He gives a grunt. "I may have a buyer for the boat."

"Miss Steak!" I exclaim. "You want to sell Miss Steak?"

"What good is it to me now? There's no-one to go out with, what with your being away all the time." He waits for me to say something, but I remain silent. "Where are you hiding, anyway? I haven't seen you going in and out down below."

"I'm not hiding anywhere. I live on the Plateau with two other guys in biology, one in my year and the other, a year behind us. It's a lot more fun, and closer to my courses and to the library."

He looks at me angrily. "What? You moved? Without telling me?" He asks me where exactly and I give him my address.

"David," he says. "I'm not happy with all this. Not happy at all. I want you to move back here with me. Now."

"Dad," I say. "Sorry, but it's out of the question. I'm grown up now. It's only normal that I should be living with my friends. I'm staying put." He glares at me and I manage to return his look without lowering my eyes. "How old were you when you first left Grandad and went to live in Montreal?" I ask him. I know the answer already. It was very close to my present age. He thinks for a moment and decides to change tack.

"Who's paying for it? Where are you getting the money from?"

"There are bursaries and student loans," I say.

"It would be less expensive if you lived here." His attack is losing its edge.

"Dad," I say. "I'm awfully thirsty. Any chance of a beer?"

"Good idea." He gets up and goes to the kitchen. When he gets back, I can see that his mood has improved somewhat.

"Did you meet any girls up there in Goose Bay? Some of them can be pretty good."

I think of Akna and decide at once that I am not going to tell him about her. "Nothing special."

He looks for a new topic of conversation. "Remember how I used to bring pizzas in from the Steak House when you were studying, and make you coffee? Do you remember that, Davie?"

I nod, and he starts to tell me about the Steak House. It seems that nothing has happened since the fire, apart from the fact that Annie has drifted off, taken a job somewhere. That doesn't seem to bother him though. "It's the damn insurers, Davie. They are so slow you couldn't believe it. And the questions they ask. When I think of the premiums which I paid over all those years, it's a disgrace, really it is."

I commiserate but can't help remembering Chip's question. *And were there footprints?* Perhaps the insurers have their reasons.

He is more relaxed now and starts quizzing me about what I did over the summer. I have to be careful. He doesn't yet know that Mum and I have made contact. I am tempted to tell him so just to get it behind me, but have promised Mum not to do so, at least not yet. "Chip and I took Grandad's ashes up to Nain," I start. "Chip flew, but I took the ferry. That was beautiful. We had a great canoe trip down a river called the Kanairiktok. I went fishing for trout on Grand Lake with a new friend called Andrew, and Chip and I visited an archeological site out near Cartwright. It was a pretty full summer, really."

"Did you go to a place called Hopedale?" he asks.

"No," I answer. "I just saw it from the ferry."

"You didn't miss much. All that sounds fine, Davie, but once you've done it once it gets pretty boring. I bet you're glad to be back in Montreal." I shrug.

"What do you make of my brother?" he asks. "A queer man. All those years in the civil service."

"We got on very well together," I reply, on my guard.

"I'll tell you what's wrong with the civil service, Davie." He leans towards me as if he is revealing a great confidence. "Someone does the work. Someone else supervises him. Then there's a committee to make sure the supervisor is doing the supervision properly. Others look on to ensure that there are enough women involved, still others to ensure the women aren't being fooled around with. Halfway through your career, you look down the corridor from your shitty little office with the brown linoleum floor and think that with a following wind, in another ten years, you'll have that other office further down the corridor with a carpet, an air conditioner and a view of the river. That," he concludes, "that is life in the civil service."

He realises that he has been carried away by his love of exaggeration, and we both laugh. However, he comes back to the charge. "You know, my brother Chip has drifted most of his life. He flunked out of university. He has never put down roots, never married. Be careful. I hate to say so, but he's not to be trusted."

I try to break in. "I disagree..." I start to say, but he interrupts me.

"That bastard of a brother of mine is challenging your grandad's will. He's trying to rob us, to rob you and me of our inheritance." He pauses for effect, then continues, speaking rapidly and with a voice that is trembling in anger.

"Grandad wasn't a poor man. When he went into the Residence - Oh, and I organised all that, David, your uncle was farting around up north somewhere - I accepted to take care of his finances. And I've done pretty well with them. There's more now than when I took over. You can be sure of that."

He nods his head energetically, and before I have time to say anything points a finger at me. "Grandad made a will thinking of you, David. He knew you would need to be provided for while you finished your studies. He saw how I was taking care of you. He was very fond of you, proud of you. So he left his money in trust, tied it up so I could take care of you until you reached thirty. That's what Grandad did. But Chip has hired a lawyer to fight that. He is trying to cheat you. That's the hard truth."

My head is ringing. He makes it all sound convincing. He has that gift of sounding sincere, of building a reality out of shadows. But I know he's lying, and his comments about my real father are making my blood boil. "Can I say something? Will you please listen to me?" I ask.

Once more he breaks in. He is on his feet now and speaking in a very loud voice. "You and I must stick together, father and son. I have some big battles coming up that are very important to me and also to you. The insurers. My brother Chip. I need your support one hundred percent. All the way. You won't let your own father down. I know you won't."

24

That autumn, I go several times to Baie-Comeau to stay with Mum for the weekend. We now have a wonderful rapport. I suppose that if you have a constant relationship with a parent, as in the normal situation, you form your common experience gradually and imperceptibly over a long period of time. With Mum, I didn't know her when I was young, nor when I was growing up. We only returned into each other's lives as adults. As a result, we have become like pals, like friends of the same approximate age, rather than like persons of two different generations.

At the same time, we are mother and son, and that adds another dimension. In a thousand different ways, she seeks to guide me, to encourage me, to nudge me in the right direction. She takes me to a clothing store to buy a sweater she feels I need. She shows me how to iron a shirt properly. She and I spend a lot of time together in the kitchen, cooking and chatting.

I get to know a host of uncles, aunts and cousins. Mum comes from a stupendous family; stupendous at least for me, an only child with nary a cousin to show on the

Forbes side. She has one brother in Forestville, another in Baie-Saint-Paul, two sisters in Lac Saint-Jean, another in Rimouski. There are cousins, nieces and nephews everywhere: hockey players, schoolteachers, policemen, crab fishermen, ballet dancers, two priests and a nun! My weekends with Mum are one long social gathering.

I can tell that she is very proud to show me around. "You know, David, they all took pity on me because my marriage had failed, because my health suffered so much. They never really saw me as a mother, as having my own family. But now I have you and that changes everything! You can't start to understand how much that changes things for me!"

Mum has a lot of friends as well, but as far as I can tell, there never was another man in her life after her failed marriage with Leo. One day she tells me as much. "It was a roller-coaster ride. Some days Leo was reasonable, even loving. Other days, he was impossible. I learned to suppress my feelings, to lead a life with my brain, but not with my heart. I built defences. Once Leo and I separated, it was an enormous relief and I swore that I would never permit myself to go through the same experience again."

She then gives a curious smile. "You know. I'm not a fatalist. Not at all. And yet there are sometimes coincidences in our lives that astonish us and make us think that...well...yes, fate can play a part in what happens to us. Let me give you an example. I have a friend who emigrated here from France. She came by boat at the age of eighteen. She married a Canadian, raised a family, was widowed, and married a second time. It turned out that she and her second husband had come out from France on the very same boat. Now there's a coincidence!"

I look at her expectantly, not seeing the relevance of her story. "David. After that night with Chip, I never expected to see him again. And yet now here he is again, back in my life. Who or what has brought this about? You of all people!" We both laugh happily.

It seems that she is another person since she and I have found each other. All her relations and friends say so. Her brother Armand, who is chief of police in Forestville, is with us one afternoon.

"David," he says to me. "You are a tonic for your mother. When you aren't here, she talks about you all the time."

"Come on, Armand," Mum says, slightly embarrassed. "That's a bit of an exaggeration."

"Not only that," he continues, "but she is now looking younger by a good twenty years." Mum blushes and gives him a big hug.

On one of my visits, I once more show Mum the photograph that Grandad kept in his papers. "Who was it who took this picture?" she asks herself, turning it over and over again.

She has a sudden thought. "There was an accountant who did things for your grandad part time. She was living in Goose Bay, but came from Montreal. Maybe she took it."

"What was her name?" I ask. She frowns and thinks hard.

"Prendergast. That's it! Miss Prendergast. She occasionally joined us at home on Grandad's visits. I think her first name was Elinore."

It is a name which I remember from somewhere. It is the sort of name which one doesn't forget easily. Perhaps I saw it in the register that we all signed at Grandad's funeral. Perhaps I had come across it in Grandad's papers.

Once back in Montreal, I look in his papers and find a mention of her name with a telephone number. It would be interesting to find out what she has to say about Grandad. Perhaps also, I will learn something that will help me discover if Leo has some sort of skeleton in his closet. Accordingly, I dial the number and a woman's voice answers. "Excuse me, but could I please speak to Elinore Prendergast?" The answer is formal. "This is she."

When I introduce myself, the formality falls and she assures me that she would be delighted to have my visit. She gives me the address of an apartment building in Montreal West, on Sherbrooke Street. We agree to meet the following Saturday.

The day is grey and a light rain is falling. In these circumstances, Montreal can look drab. Rain in the country suggests life and renewal, but in the city, it means raincoats and umbrellas.

The apartment building is a large and very solid-looking red brick building, probably dating back to the nineteen-twenties. There are heavy oak doors with brass studs and double-glazed windows, and an antiquated elevator which leads up to the third floor. On the door to Miss Prendergast's apartment is a heavy brass knocker, an effigy of William Shakespeare. It seems to have been polished recently and gleams brightly against the dark oak door. I sound it and an echo reverberates within. The door opens almost immediately.

Miss Prendergast stands there, her short grey hair tied up in a bun. She is dressed in a long black dress and looks the part of a retired spinster chartered accountant, if there is such a part. She is slim, not very tall, impeccable, precise, and ageless.

Her apartment is small and orderly. The entry hall is windowless and lit by a wall sconce of gilt cherubs. Further on is a living room dominated by a cut-glass chandelier, a worn oriental carpet and a grandfather clock. The clock is ticking noisily. I have the feeling that it has just been wound up and is feeling its oats.

I perch on the edge of a blue Victorian settee as she examines me. "Tea?" she asks. "That would be very nice," I reply, and she produces a silver tea service from the adjacent kitchen, the teapot steaming beside two porcelain cups and a plate of digestive biscuits.

I ask her about Grandad. "Did you always see him in Goose Bay?"

"Of course," she answers. "I never had to go up to Nain. We corresponded often, and he occasionally came down to Goose Bay. I was working in a small accountancy practice at the time, but my employer didn't mind if I worked evenings, which I did occasionally for your grandfather and for others."

It was unusual hearing about Grandad from a stranger. I ask what she did for him. "Letters. He would dictate letters. I paid his bills. I also made his travel arrangements."

She thinks for a while. "Your grandfather was a good man. I remember once when a man working with him on a construction site had an accident. His arm was crushed by a piece of heavy equipment. I think he was from New Brunswick. Did you ever hear of that?" I say "No".

"He came down to Goose Bay with the injured man. A surgeon from Montreal did three operations, but after a week the man died. They couldn't stop him from losing blood. All that time your grandfather visited the man in hospital, giving him encouragement. After the man died, your grandfather passed the hat around the other men working at the site and raised close to nineteen hundred dollars for the man's widow back in New Brunswick. He then rounded it up to five thousand. I know. It was I who arranged for the money to be transferred to the widow."

"Was it you who took this photo?" I show her the one of Grandad with Leo, Chip and Valérie.

She smiles in recognition. "Yes! I remember that. We were at Leo and Valérie's." She turns the photo over. "See. That's my writing."

We chat along for quite a while and I guide our conversation to the moment when Grandad came south to visit Leo and Mum when they were about to move to Montreal. "Tell me how Grandad felt about their leaving."

"He seemed preoccupied. I remember that he delayed his departure for the north by a day or two and then instead of returning to Nain as he had previously intended, left for Hopedale. I had to change the booking for him."

"Was that unusual?"

"Well, yes, in fact. He rarely returned to Nain via Hopedale. He told me it was important. He seemed annoyed, worried even. Seemingly, something had happened up there. I never did understand what it was about."

I finish my tea and thank Miss Prendergast. "I apologise for not talking to you at the funeral," she says. "Normally, I would have. However - and I'm sorry to say so - I wanted to avoid your father. He and I never quite saw eye to eye."

25

It is early November, and as I have a week off from university, I go up to Goose Bay to stay with Dad. We talk about Mum a lot, and he also tells me that his lawyer has uncovered a number of abuses in the way that Leo administered Grandad's finances in the years preceding his death. "Believe me," he says. "I don't have much use for money, but I do take objection when someone tries to take me for a ride."

After two days, he is unexpectedly called off to Ottawa. "I'm really sorry, but I have no choice. What would you like to do while I'm away?"

It doesn't take me a second to reply. "Makkovik. I would like to visit Makkovik."

He gives me an amused look. "Makkovik. Well, that's a nice enough idea. You're hoping to meet up with that girl, I suppose. Why not? How will you go?"

"By plane. Or the ferry. Depending on what's available."

We make enquiries and it turns out that the ferry is leaving the next day. Because of some previous bad weather, not uncommon in November, it is off schedule and is now operating on what they call "load and go". I decide to take the ferry.

The weather is rough, but the *Northern Ranger* braves the elements and in two days' time I find myself with a small packsack disembarking at Makkovik. Leaving the wharf area, I start to look around.

I really have no plan as to where to stay and what to do. As it happens, the local hotel is right there in front of me. It is very neat and tidy, so I take a room and leaving my bag there, go for a walk around town.

It is a beautifull, sunny day and the season's first snow is lying sparkling on the ground. The villagers are very friendly. Just one look and they can tell I'm a stranger. One old-timer examines me as he is fiddling with a ski-doo outside his house. He is wearing a bulky winter jacket and orange waterproof pants, and his face is worn and a bit puffy under the eyes. "Won't be long now," he says to me.

"What is your favourite season?" I ask with a smile, expecting him to launch into a bitter complaint about the winter, but not a bit of it.

"Oh, winter," is the reply. "Easily! We get all kinds of snow and don't plow the roads. Everyone gets about on a ski-doo like this one here. I can't wait."

Further along, a man hails me from the steps to a shed beside his house. We have a good chat, and he explains to me that he was a fisherman but is retired now and still does a bit of netting in the bay for char and trout. His quad bike is parked nearby and a harpoon sticks out of the box at its back. "To catch a seal once it's dead," he explains. "Otherwise, they sometimes sink."

Back in the centre of the village I come across an oil drum turned into a public refuse bin. It has been brightly painted and carries the message *HAVE FUN; BOAT*

SAFE; DON'T LITTER. I reach into my pocket and in goes a plastic bottle I picked up earlier by the roadside.

By now, I am getting a bit cold and the day is wearing on, so I return to the hotel for a hot shower and some supper. So far, no luck in my search for Akna.

The next morning, I leave the hotel and continue to explore Makkovik. At the local handicraft store, I buy Mum a magnificent pair of sealskin mitts, trimmed with white arctic hare fur. I will give them to her for Christmas.

I visit the local museum, a handsome white clapboard building called The *White Elephant,* so called because it was originally intended to be a school dormitory attached to the Moravian mission, but immediately proved too small. Inside, a number of relics of life on the Labrador coast are on display.

Beside it is the Moravian church, surprisingly large for a village of three hundred. My thoughts wander in that little church; to think of all the emotions that must have been aroused here, all the weddings and all the funerals!

Walking back through the village, I see signs of unusual activity along the water's edge. A man is unloading scrap lumber from his pickup truck. "It's Bonfire Night tonight," he says with a grin as he throws the wood onto a pile beside the truck. "Guy Somebody. Every year, we do this at the start of November."

Nearby is a small multi-coloured shed with a sort of tower and widow's walk stuck on its side. A mammoth woodpile is growing on the rocks beyond it. "Tonight, there will be bonfires all along here," I am told.

Beside the next stack of wood is a life-sized figure made out of blue coveralls stuffed with small branches and dried grass. It is wearing red rubber gloves and an old pair of boots, and the head is made from an old rag rolled up into a ball with big buttons for the eyes. A man stands there putting finishing touches to it. "I'm putting a bit of gunpowder inside," he jokes. "Wasn't there something to do with gunpowder?" I laugh, shrugging my shoulders. "In any event, the kids will love it," he says.

"When will you light them all?" I ask.

"As soon as it gets dark. Around five or six. The whole of Makkovik will be down here by then. Be sure you don't miss it."

Back at the hotel, I am overcome by an unusual sensation. It is a feeling of anticipation, a sense that something big is about to happen to me. I suddenly know that Akna and I will meet this same evening. How will it go? What will she be like? Am I right to attach so much importance to our meeting? What direction will my life take after we do meet? Am I at a major turning point?

I take out the amulet, and it gives me confidence. "Go for it," it seems to tell me. "Don't look back. Take the right decisions and everything will work out."

I am still immersed in these thoughts when I leave the hotel. The bonfires are now in full flame, sending their sparks curling up into the black sky above. Around them, groups of figures move in and out of the shadows, holding mugs of hot chocolate and fresh donuts.

I visit one group after another and eventually come to the multi-coloured shed where a place is made for me close by the fire. Some teenagers standing on the other side of the fire have noticed my presence and seem to be discussing me. There is a lot of shoving and laughter, and as I watch, a tall girl with long black braids wearing a pale blue ski jacket puts a marshmallow on the end of a stick and crouching by the fire roasts it carefully. She then stands up, and urged on by two of her friends, walks over and offers the marshmallow to me. My heart skips a beat. It is Akna.

"This is for you," she says almost inaudibly, quickly handing me the stick with the marshmallow on it and returning to her group. They all break out into laughter, and one or two of them clap. The fire gives out a great burst of sparks as I swallow the marshmallow. "Thanks," I call across to her, but her back is already turned. I am furious with myself. This was my first meeting with her, and I completely missed my chance. What a wimp!

Fortunately for me, an older woman whom I recognise as her mother is watching and comes to speak to me. "Was it good?" she asks of the marshmallow, looking me over. She must like what she sees, for she returns to the girl and says to her, "Akna. Come with me." The two come over to where I am standing, the young girl reluctantly. "This is my daughter, Akna," the girl's mother says proudly. "What is your name?"

"I am David, David Forbes."

"Where are you from?" the mother asks. "What brings you here?" Akna is pretending not to listen, but I can feel her eyes on me.

"I'm from Montreal. My grandfather used to live up here and my grandmother was from Newfoundland, so I came for a visit. I go back on the boat to Goose Bay tomorrow."

"You're lucky," says the mother, "being here for Bonfire Night."

"Yes," I say. "It's a lot of fun. I hadn't expected it at all."

"Do you like it in Labrador?"

Here, I am able to let my feelings go. "I love it," I say. "Particularly up here." The mother clearly approves.

Akna has been holding herself apart from us, but now takes a step closer. "Why?" she asks in a soft, slightly childish voice. I smile at her in the light of the fire as our eyes meet for the first time.

"Because there is so much space, because the land is so beautiful, because there is so much future."

She frowns. "There is also much past. Our people have lived here for a long time. We have our language, our customs."

I feel slightly stupid. "I'm sorry. I didn't wish to suggest the contrary. I know I have much to learn."

At this point, Akna's mother leaves us and Akna herself starts to edge towards her former group. "I hope that we can meet again," I manage to say. "Can we see each other sometime?"

She laughs a little laugh. "Maybe," she says, and turns away.

26

I am having difficulty getting to sleep. The room is too hot. I open the window wide. Just as I am getting really drowsy, the wind picks up outside. My feet start getting cold. I close the window.

No sooner am I back in bed than I need to go to the bathroom.

Up I get. Returning from the bathroom, I look at my watch. It is two in the morning. Perhaps I have slept, perhaps not. Once more, the room is too hot. I can't decide which side to sleep on. Face to the wall or face to the room?

It's all because of Akna. I can't think of anything other than her. It's crazy, but that's just the way it is.

Early next morning, I lie in bed talking to myself. "My ferry's in two hours' time. Should I go? If I stay, will she speak to me? Would I just be wasting my time? If I leave, when will I find my way back to Makkovik? I'm here. Surely, I should stay." I continue the debate in my mind, but in my heart of hearts the debate has already produced a winner. I'm staying.

The owner of the hotel helps me cancel the ferry

booking and reserve a flight to Goose Bay at the end of the day. He also tells me with a private smile where Akna lives. When I leave the hotel, it is ten o'clock on a cold, but sunny morning. The recent fresh snow still lies on the ground. This time I am determined. I will risk all!

The road along the water's edge leads out towards the open sea. At the end, a small neat house stands apart amongst some stunted spruce. Outside, I can see a snowmobile propped up on one side and a figure lying on a sheet of cardboard under it, dressed in navy-blue overalls and holding a large spanner. "Excuse me," I ask. "Does Akna live here?"

The person looks up from under the machine. "Who, me?" She has a dark smudge of grease on her cheek and a tuque pulled way down over her hair, but I recognise her at once.

"Hello, Akna. It's me again. David. You want a hand?"

"I'm just changing the engine oil, but the nut is too tight."

"Let me try." I get down on the cardboard beside her on my knees. I tell myself that this is to be the decisive moment. If I succeed, I will win her forever. If I fail...

"Hang on," she says, lying there beside me and handing me the spanner. She shoves a decapitated plastic container under the machine. "That's to catch the oil."

I succeed. The nut loosens, and together we open it slowly and allow the container to fill. My hands are covered with oil, but I have never felt so happy in my life! For the next few minutes, we minister together to the snowmobile. All this time, she barely looks at me. "Thanks," she says at the end, wiping her machine proudly with a large rag. "This is the fastest snowmobile in Makkovik."

"You have some grease on your cheek," I tell her, pulling out a handkerchief. "Let me."

She tilts up her face to me and I start to wipe the grease off her cheek. Our eyes meet. At first hers is a steady look. But as I continue, it changes to a questioning look, next to a puzzled look, finally to a fleeting, but dreamy look. We both look down. My heart is bursting. "Can we go for a walk?"

"OK," she says. "I'll go in and clean up."

When she returns, we set out on our walk. "Aren't you taking the ferry back?"

"No, I'm on this afternoon's plane."

"I thought you came on the ferry."

"I did."

"So why aren't you on it now?"

"I changed my mind." There is a pause. "I wanted to see you again."

"Why?"

"I just did," I manage to say. "Do you know what? This is the third time we have met."

"No," she corrects me. "Twice. Yesterday and today."

"And once in Montreal."

"How come?"

We take the road that goes up the hillside towards the school. I start to explain to her how Grandad used to send me over to a hostel with his spare cash, and how we once met when she was staying there with her grandmother. The day is getting warmer and I undo the top buttons of my coat. "He must be a good man, your grandfather."

"He was. He died last winter."

"I'm sorry. I have a very special grandfather, but he too is getting old. He lives with us in the house. What did you think of our bonfires last night?"

"That was fun. Everyone outside enjoying themselves." I then add in what I think is a burst of gallantry "I particularly liked the marshmallows!"

She looks at me. "You're too fast. Don't forget, I live here. You are just visiting." I try to apologise, but she brushes it aside. "This is a small community. We stick together. We are suspicious of strangers."

We turn off to the left and take the boardwalk that leads along the hillside above the village. It is slippery in places where the fresh snow has melted and turned to ice. In places, she goes ahead of me. Her long black braids hang out from under a blue tuque.

"You seem to like blue," I say. "Every time I see you, you're in blue."

She reflects. "You may be right. Most of my things are blue. You notice things. Are you going to be an artist?"

I laugh. "I'm hopeless at drawing. No. I want to become a doctor."

Her eyes widen. "That's good," she says.

"And you?"

"An author. I sometimes write poetry."

"Would you show some to me?"

She laughs. "I'm not sure. It's mostly in our language. You wouldn't understand it."

"Perhaps you could read it to me. That way, I could listen to your voice, watch your face."

She looks down. "You still wouldn't understand it."

We reach the highest point of the boardwalk and admire the views out over the inlet and village lying at our feet. Again, our eyes meet and I can read in hers a mixture of hesitation and curiosity. It is as if my intrusion into her life gives her pleasure, but is at the same time unwelcome. For my part, I am overwhelmed; I have never felt like this before. "This so beautiful," I say with a wave of the hand, indicating the broad rounded hill across on the other side of the inlet. She simply nods.

We start down the further side, where the boardwalk

descends to the road leading back towards the village. I am doing most of the talking, telling her about my life in Montreal, my mother in Baie- Comeau, my father in Goose Bay. Not knowing what to say about Leo, I leave him out. I then hit on the idea of telling her about my canoe trip down the Kanairiktok.

"That must have been fun," she says. "I'd like to do that one day. By canoe, I mean. I've been there lots by ski-doo. The big falls are beautiful when they freeze."

"That's a long way to go by ski-doo," I say. "You make trips like that?"

"In the winter, we can go more places than in summer. It's faster as well. There are trails that go to Hopedale, Goose Bay. Even to Nain. Then there's also the ice to travel on."

"As long as you don't run into a polar bear," I joke.

She looks at me. "Oh, we do. My uncle once shot one and ended up three months in the hospital in Goose Bay."

"How come? What happened?"

Akna gives me a very serious look. "Do you really want me to tell you?" She doesn't wait for an answer. "This was many years ago. A male bear came down the coast on the ice. The villagers saw his tracks in the snow out in the bay. They were very big tracks. The school was down here then and the parents were too frightened to let their children go to school alone. My uncle had a permit and went out on his snowmobile with a *Komatik* behind. He followed the tracks out there on the ice and saw the bear. It stood up and sniffed the air, and then started towards my uncle. It was very big. Like this." She reaches her hand as high in the air as she can.

"Keep going," I say willingly. "What happened next?"

"My uncle took a first shot. The bear stood up and scratched his chest with his big paw. He started to run forward. My uncle was a brave hunter and just stood there. He took a second shot. The bear jumped sideways but kept coming closer. It was really angry now. My uncle took a third shot. The bear collapsed at his feet." Akna waves her hand dramatically at my feet.

"It was very cold out there on the ice and the wind was blowing, but my uncle got out his big knife and skinned the bear. He removed the best parts to eat. He loaded the *Komatik* with the skin and the meat and returned to the village." Akna waves a hand in the direction of the village down the hill to our left. "He was very proud."

"He came into the village at top speed and did a flying stop, the one where you turn the ski-doo hard to one side. Just down there by the wharf. The *Komatik* came sliding around in the snow and turned upside down, spilling the bear skin and the meat out onto the road. There were some sled dogs there that weren't tied up. They smelled the blood of the bear on the *Komatik* and on my uncle's clothes and it drove them crazy. They jumped on him and bit him all over. Some men were nearby and saved him. Then he had to go down to the hospital in Goose Bay for quite a while."

We stand there in silence, and she turns to face me with a smile. "Did you like the story, David?"

I immediately sense the meaning of her smile and laugh. "I loved it. Did it really happen, mummy?"

She reaches out an arm and gives me a quick tug at the waist. "I made it up, just for you."

From then on, our day passes as if in a dream. At least it does for me. We walk and walk, Akna becoming ever more talkative. I learn about her family, her friends, the teachers at school, politics in Makkovik. It is marvellous.

When it comes time for me to catch my plane, she takes me out to the landing strip on her quad bike. I sit behind, my arms wrapped around her waist as she takes each turn of the road like a racing car driver. Our parting is rapid as the plane has already arrived from the north and is preparing to leave. I would like to kiss her, but she doesn't let me. Long afterwards, I can still feel her body just ahead of mine, with my arms wrapped around her waist.

"Akna?" I am calling her from Montreal two weeks later. "How are you?"

"It's snowing," is her laconic answer. "Here too," I say.

Our phone calls are difficult. She doesn't want to chat and make idle conversation. For her, a long-distance call is an extravagance and should be kept as short and businesslike as possible. Perhaps she is also embarrassed at receiving my calls at home.

"Can I come and see you next weekend?" I ask her. I have no plan, no knowledge of how I can get from Montreal to Makkovik for a weekend. All I know is that I want to see her again. I must see her. It has become the most important and compelling thing in my life.

"Yes," is the answer. I detect a trace of warmth in her voice and am encouraged.

"I'll come then."

"See you then," she says and rings off, leaving me impotent at the other end of the line.

After a seemingly endless series of plane trips and

airport changes, I find myself in Makkovik at about midday on the Saturday. I get a lift from the little landing strip to the hotel where I am by now well known. "You are invited to Akna's at five," I am told. "There is to be a storytelling."

That afternoon, I walk over to Akna's house at five, not knowing what to expect and disappointed that she and I are not already somewhere alone, sharing our precious time together. It is already getting dark and there is a bite in the air. Akna's mother opens the door for me, and with a warm smile leads me through to the kitchen where six or eight persons are gathered about a wood stove in semi-darkness. The room is warm, a bit of softwood smoke lingers in the air and the atmosphere is one of expectation.

I take the chair which is offered to me, beside Akna, who greets me somewhat formally. "We're going to listen to one of my grandfather's stories. It's a special thing in our family."

"Thank you," I say. "You are very kind to include me." She nods.

On her other side is a very old man whom I take to be her grandfather. He seems to be blind. Closing the circle are Akna's grandmother, who is apparently her mother's mother, and a middle-aged couple who could be an aunt and uncle. I am offered some tea.

Akna turns to me and in a soft melodious voice that I have now come to recognise tells me that her grandfather is called Ittuq, and that he is her mother's father. He was born in the north, at Hebron, and likes to tell old stories about how life once was for the Inuit. "They are never the same from one time to the next, so it's hard to translate, but I'll do my best."

We wait for a while in silence and the old man finally starts, speaking Inuktitut in short sentences and a low monotone. Akna translates, speaking slowly and making a

special effort to enunciate clearly as a schoolteacher would
with small children.

"This was told me by my grandfather," he starts.

The ice is flat and thick
Snow crystals on the ice
The man shades his eyes.

The sun is low and distant
Three sleds are coming
Nuthak the trader.

Akna raises her hand to ask her grandfather to pause.
She turns to me. "Can you understand?" I nod. The hand
comes down, and Ittuq continues slowly.

Nuthak has sixteen dogs
Sixteen dogs to pull his sleds
With baleen and walrus tusks.

They knock the man to the ice
And the woman too
On the flat ice.

They take his baleen
And seize the girl
They break the igloo.

They hold up a child by one foot
Nuthak raises his hand
No! The child can live.

They travel two moons
Two moons to the south
To trade with the white man.

To where the Innu go
To where the seals gather
To trade baleen and tusks.

There follows a silence which no one wishes to break.

Ittuq has finished his story and we are all digesting its elements, visualising the events as they unfolded.

Akna serves everyone more tea and various conversations break out in the room. I turn to her. "Tell me, Akna. What was the meaning of the last verse? Where did the trader go?" I'm thinking of the moment when Grandad gave me the amulet, and when I asked of its source answered "where the seals gather". Perhaps there is a connection.

She frowns. "I'm not sure. I'll ask Ittuq." She does so. "He says that there were many places where the Inuit traders went to trade."

"But what does he mean by 'Where the Innu go. Where the seals gather'?"

Once more, she asks Ittuq. She shrugs. "It could be many places."

I turn in my chair. It is a kitchen chair and none too comfortable. I can feel the amulet in my pocket and decide to show it to Akna and the others. "Look at this. My Grandad gave this to me just before he died. I think it must come from somewhere up near Nain, where he worked."

"It is unusual," she says, turning the amulet over in her hands. Her mother is watching and asks to see the amulet. It is then passed around from hand to hand, each time eliciting a comment or an exclamation.

When it is finally put in Ittuq's hands, he feels it slowly with the intense concentration of someone who is blind. He rotates it carefully, his fingertips probing it at every point. Conversation in the room stops. We are all watching the old man. Once more, he starts to speak and once more, Akna translates for me in her low voice.

"When I was young," he says, "I worked on a fishing boat. We fished for cod. The fishing was good. I lived in Hopedale. I worked like that for three years. My wife was from Nain. Together, we had two daughters. Akna's mother was the older daughter. Sadie was the younger one." I begin to sense a certain unease in the room.

"The weather that year was bad. There came a big storm. The waves were too much for our boat. They were breaking over the bow, pushing us towards the rocks. We only just reached Smokey in time. There is good protection there."

"We tied up at the wharf at Smokey. We were tired and hungry. There was another boat there, tied up on the other side of the wharf. It was also a fishing boat."

"The crew of the other boat asked us over to eat and to drink. I was young. I didn't decide. Our skipper did. We went to the other boat and ate something."

"Crewing on the other boat was an Inuk. His initials were BG. That's what the others called him. They called him BG." At this point, one person starts to whisper to the others in the room. It is a very audible whisper, and there is a certain degree of nervous shuffling and coughing.

"On the fishing boat, BG carved stone. He carved it beautifully. In the old style, the old manner. He gave me a piece which he had just finished making. It was a gift. It was a head, like this one."

"When she was still young, I gave the head to my daughter Sadie..."

Ittuq begins to cry, silently, the tears running down his cheeks. I have no idea why he is crying, but the atmosphere in the room has become so heavy that I could just about crawl into a corner and die. We all wait expectantly, but Ittuq is too overcome to continue.

Akna's grandmother starts to talk. Once more, Akna translates. "We were living in Hopedale. He went out three days in his boat on Ugjoktok Bay looking for her. When he came back with Sadie's body, his face was so swollen and bruised you couldn't see his eyes. In his grief he had hit himself in the face, out there in the boat, first with his hands, then with an oar."

"If you have never lost a child, you can't understand such grief."

There is more silence, more silent even than silence. At a certain moment, Ittuq closes the evening. "The amulet will protect you when you take the right decisions. But if you take wrong decisions, no amulet will protect you."

Akna and I walk back to the hotel together in silence. The drama of Ittuq's story and of Sadie's death has overwhelmed us. "Tell me about Sadie," I ask of Akna.

"She was my mother's sister," is the reply, "but I never knew her. She died before I was born."

"Her story is very sad," I say.

"Yes, very sad. I have never heard Ittuq tell it before. At least, not like that." When we reach the hotel, she turns her cheek to me for a kiss and we agree to remain in touch, but the mood is sombre and it seems to me that in some way, Sadie's tragic end has come between us.

28

Christmas in Goose Bay. I stare out the window of the plane at the Mealy Mountains, their eroded summits glistening white in the bright sunshine. Returning to Labrador makes me think of Akna and I get a worried feeling in the pit of my stomach. I remember Ittuq's story of Sadie's death, and how Akna and I both felt when last we saw each other. Is it even worthwhile trying to get in touch with her?

Mum and Dad meet me at the airport, waving enthusiastically, and we go home in Dad's green pickup. The snow is everywhere, filling the ditches, drifting gently across the roads, piled high around the buildings.

Dad is bursting to tell me something, I can tell. You can see the excitement on his face. As we reach the house, he can wait no longer. "We're engaged, David! Your Mum has said 'yes'." Mum removes her gloves and proudly shows me a diamond ring, tilting her hand back and forth to make it flash in my eyes.

I am genuinely pleased for them, and suddenly swept by the realisation that their marriage will somehow, and

195

oh so conveniently, regularise my own situation. "That's wonderful. I'm really happy for you both." They smile at each other and look slightly self-conscious. "Better late than never," says Dad with a grin. "I never thought I'd do this again," adds my mother.

Mum has been there for a week, tidying and rearranging things, cooking and baking, singing songs while she bustles about. It is a marvel to see what she has done with Dad's house. There are little changes, little touches everywhere.

She insists that we go to midnight Mass. "It's not that I am all that religious, David, but I am Québecoise, you are my son and the Catholic Church is a part of our culture." Fortunately, my French is pretty good. Otherwise, I think she would be sending me off to night courses. She is taking her new role as mother very seriously!

On Christmas morning, I help Mum in the kitchen. Never before did I know how to glaze a turnip or braise endives in white wine, and it is certainly the first time that I have ever stuffed a goose with prunes filled with foie gras.

Lunch is delicious and we celebrate together around the table. After the pudding, we open our presents. From Dad, I receive a book on Taoism, and from Mum, a pair of green corduroy trousers. I proudly present Mum with the mitts I bought for her in Makkovik, and Dad, with a few fishing flies. The day wears on and we are happy and united.

Mum asks me about my visit to Makkovik in November. She particularly wants to hear about Akna. "She sounds wonderful. Are you going to try to see her again this trip?"

"Oh, Mum," I say, "I'm not sure."

"Why not?" Mum and Dad both ask at the same time.

I tell them what happened. "I was invited to a special

evening at her house. Her grandfather told an old story and she translated it for me. I then pulled out the amulet to show them. The grandfather, even though he is blind, recognised it as being similar to one that he once had given to his younger daughter, a girl called Sadie. Akna's aunt, in effect. Apparently, Sadie drowned and I guess my amulet made him think of his daughter's death. It all happened before Akna was born, but I could tell that the event was still very alive in everyone's mind."

"How sad," Mum says. "But does that prevent you from seeing Akna again?"

"It was very awkward, my pulling out the amulet and her grandfather making the connection between it and his daughter who drowned."

"Do they know how she drowned?"

"Not that I know of," I answer.

"When was it?"

"It must have been about twenty years ago, since Akna wasn't born yet. Maybe a bit more."

"Have you told them that your amulet originally came from your uncle Leo?" Mum wants to know.

"No, I haven't. But it seems as though the two amulets, mine and the one the grandfather gave to his daughter Sadie, were carved by the same man, a man called BG. I suppose it's even possible that the two amulets are one and the same."

We fall silent. The same thought is occurring to each of us: that Leo may have known Sadie and somehow obtained the amulet from her.

"At least give Akna a call to wish her Happy New Year. She won't bite you!" Mum suggests.

"Maybe. We'll see," I answer.

The next day, Dad and I discuss how matters stand as regards Grandad's estate. I relate how Leo told me that he was counting on my support in both his dispute with the insurer and in that over Grandad's will.

Dad is not surprised. "My lawyer is ready to bring proceedings. He thinks that we have an excellent chance of having the second will annulled on the basis that Grandad was no longer sound of mind. What bothers me, though, is that you would almost certainly have to testify. After all, you saw a lot of Grandad during his last years. If we didn't call you as a witness, Leo would certainly do so."

We discuss what this would mean. In fact, the whole relationship with Leo looks like it is going to get very messy. Sooner or later, he is going to learn that Dad and Mum intend to get married. His brother with his former wife! That will certainly make him see red.

Then if we go to court, the credibility of my evidence concerning Grandad will become an issue. Am I partial? At that point, are we not obliged to reveal to the court that my real father is Dad, not Leo? How will Leo react to that little bit of information?

To top it all off, it is clear that in the course of administering Grandad's affairs, Leo helped himself on more than one occasion out of Grandad's brokerage and bank accounts. This too would have to come out in any court case. It could expose Leo to criminal charges.

"David," says Dad. "It's a complete mess. Clear as can be. What isn't clear is how we all get out of it." He gives a sigh. "I just don't know!"

I don't know either, but the whole discussion makes me realise that I no longer have the option of remaining on reasonable terms with Leo. I have to choose sides. In fact, I already have. Leo's acts, his lies and half-truths, his treatment of my mother all count against him. As far as I'm concerned, he's a stranger.

One evening that week, George Walker drops in with

his wife for a drink. We discuss his most recent finds in Sandwich Bay and on Huntingdon Island. "Next summer," George says "I have a new site that I want to explore. A very large sod house at the mouth of the North River. I think that it must have belonged to an important trader."

"European?" I ask. "Was the trader European?"

"No. An Inuit trader. They used to come down from the far north with their sleds full of precious goods that the Europeans and Innu wanted to buy, and barter them for European goods such as knife blades, harpoon tips, beads, and so forth. They would then return north over the ice and take these goods up to the Inuit populations there, again for trade."

I immediately think of Ittuq's tale and recount it to George. He gets quite excited. "I should send a team up there," he says.

"Up where?" Dad and I both ask.

"To Adlatok Bay. Because of those two lines at the end of the story: 'To where the Innu go; to where the seals gather'."

I get really excited. Will I finally find out what Grandad meant? "What do they mean?" I ask. "Those last two lines."

George smiles. "The river Adlatok is just south of Hopedale. It is a strange river. About thirty kilometres before reaching the sea it divides into two, the northern branch flowing into Adlatok Bay and the other branch, also called the Ugjoktok River, flowing into Ugjoktok Bay."

He continues. "Some people think that the word Adlatok derives from *allak*, the Inuit word for the other people of Labrador, the Innu. They would have travelled down the Adlatok River from the interior where they normally lived, perhaps specifically in order to trade with the Inuit. Similarly, I have heard it said that the word

Ugjoktok refers to a place where the *ujjuk*, or bearded seal, was to be found."

"So when he said to me 'where the seals gather', Grandad could have been referring to Ugjoktok Bay," I say. Dad nods his head in agreement. We both remain silent, turning this little bit of information over in our minds.

One morning two days before I am due to return to Montreal, I look up Akna's number and after a thousand hesitations give her a call. "Hello," says a man's voice that I don't recognise. "Whom would you like to speak to, please?"

"Akna," I answer. "I'm a friend, David Forbes. I wanted to wish her Happy New Year."

"Sorry," comes the answer. "She's down in Goose Bay visiting her uncle. Would you like her number there?" Without waiting for a reply, he gives me her number and I write it down on a scrap of paper.

29

I dial the number. My heart is thumping. It gives off a sort of ache in my chest. Will Akna agree to see me? What will be her reaction to my call?

"Hello," is the answer. It is her voice. Of that, I am sure. Slightly musical, bell-like really.

I try to sound casual. "It's David, Akna. I wanted to wish you a Happy New Year."

She laughs. "That's nice of you. Where are you?"

"In Goose Bay visiting my father."

"Your father lives in Goose Bay?" She sounds genuinely surprised. "I guess you told me, but I had forgotten."

"Yes, my father has lived in Goose Bay for the last two years now and I am up visiting him for Christmas. My mother is with us as well."

"How did you get my number?"

"I called your home in Makkovik, and someone gave it to me. He said that you were visiting an uncle in Goose Bay."

"Yes, I am."

I take a deep breath. "Could we go for a walk together?"

There is a moment of hesitation. "If you like," she answers.

We agree to meet in the parking lot in front of Maxwell's restaurant down in the centre of Goose Bay at two in the afternoon. Not a very romantic choice! Inevitably, I leave Dad's house twenty minutes too early and she arrives at Maxwell's half an hour late, by which time I am freezing. She is far better dressed for the beginnings of winter than I am.

We set out along the Hamilton River Road. "I thought you lived in Montreal," Akna says, "but here you are in Labrador for Christmas. Do you spend much time here?"

"More and more. I was brought up by an uncle in Montreal and until recently didn't know my mother and my father. Now I'm seeing a lot more of them. My father lives here in Goose Bay, and my mother, who lives in Baie-Comeau, is also here visiting him for Christmas."

Akna frowns as she attempts to digest my family history. "Do you like Goose Bay?" she finally asks.

"Yes," I say, "and you?"

"Of course," she replies emphatically. "Makkovik is so small. We all know each other. Here I can shop, see friends, all that." She looks at me. "You know, I don't even know your age. How old are you?"

"Twenty," I answer.

"I'm almost nineteen." We stand to one side as a big snowplow rattles by, scattering grit on the roadway.

"How is your grandfather?" I ask her.

"Ittuq? He is failing slowly," she says, with sadness. "I have been collecting his stories. I hope to publish them one day. Where does your father live? Where is his house here in Goose Bay?"

"On Lethbridge Street. Where does your uncle live?"

"Near there. On Learning. Let's turn here then."

We leave the Hamilton River Road and walk along a residential street. "What did you do for Christmas? Do you go to church?"

"Not normally," I reply, "but this time my mother insisted. We went to the Catholic church. Did you go to church?"

"No," she laughs. "I only go for weddings and funerals. What are you studying? Do you still want to become a doctor?"

I tell her all about my studies and my plans, and then ask about hers.

"I hope to go to Memorial University next year to study literature. My mother is afraid, though. She thinks I'll never return. This is my last year at school in Makkovik. I also teach a bit."

"You teach?"

"Well, not really teach. I do coaching at school for other students, mostly younger ones who need a bit of extra help."

"That's good of you!" I exclaim.

"When do you return to Montreal?"

"On the day after tomorrow. And you to Makkovik?"

"Next week. My uncle's house is this way." As we turn up the street to our left we have to navigate a deep drift of snow, and I reach out to take her hand. Our eyes meet. She blushes and looks down. "Why do you want to see me, David? Why do you keep coming back to me?"

I have her hand in mine. It isn't particularly romantic because we both are wearing heavy mitts. "Akna," I say. "There is something very special about you. I can't help it. It's just the way I feel."

She doesn't seem surprised, but searches for an appropriate reply. "You don't know me really, and I don't know you. It is too soon. But I like you, David." She frowns and then looks up at me. "Yes," she repeats, "I like you a lot."

This gives me the courage to bring up the subject of Sadie's death and the amulet. "Akna," I say. "There is something that bothers me."

"What is that?" She looks alarmed.

"Your aunt Sadie's death. The amulet she used to wear could have been the same one as my amulet. It was given to me by my grandfather, but once belonged to my uncle, the one who brought me up in Montreal. Maybe he knew Sadie. That is what is bothering me."

"I thought a bit about that myself," she says, "but I wasn't even born at the time. Maybe you weren't either. I can't see why we should have to worry about that."

"Are you sure?"

"Yes."

We come to a one-floor bungalow with a big garage on one side. A black pickup truck is parked in front. When we reach the front door there is a moment of hesitation, then she turns to me and reaches her arms out. We come together. She raises her face to mine and our lips meet for just a second. Nothing more. But for me it is incredible and I go into a daze of happiness.

"Can we see each other again before I leave?" I ask her.

"Tomorrow, yes. Tonight, I can't. Come here tomorrow. It would be best in the afternoon. Around two." I promise to do so.

Arriving back at Chip's home I try to appear normal, but Mum doesn't take long to uncover my secret. "That was a long walk," she says. "Did you enjoy yourselves?" I mumble something and add that I am a bit cold and need to go for a shower.

The next afternoon when I return, the black pickup

truck is gone and Akna and I go for a walk. She is looking wonderful, and her long hair falls free below her tuque. No braids today! By now, we are beginning to act as though we really know each other. We laugh together and make jokes. We walk arm in arm.

I am subjected to a long series of questions about my life as a student, how much money it costs me, what do I do when I'm not studying, whether I have a girlfriend, and so forth. "What are the girls like in Montreal?" she wants to know. I start to explain, and it soon becomes clear that what she really wants to know is whether the girls go to bed with their boyfriends or whether they wait until they are married. I answer as best I can.

When we return from our walk, she invites me into the house. It is warm and comfortable, and we sit together on a sofa facing a cast-iron wood stove that is generating a lot of heat. She is wearing blue jeans and a white T-shirt decorated with pink and blue balloons. Her nipples show softly through the fabric. This is the first time that I have seen her in ordinary house clothes. She looks beautiful, and I tell her so.

She reacts with a nervous smile, brushing her hair back behind one ear.

As we sit there, she continues with her questions about life in the big city. Do my friends still live at home? What do we do when we go out on dates? Who pays when we go out together? How many girlfriends have I had and what were they like? "Do the girls drink alcohol?" she asks. "Do you take drugs?"

Then comes the big surprise. "Do your friends have tattoos? Do you have one?"

I laugh. "No, Akna, I don't have a tattoo. Are you disappointed?"

"That's alright. I have one. It's very small. Look here."

She bares her left arm, and there at the top just by her shoulder is a tiny rose. I bend over and give it a little kiss, quickly, before she has the time to fend me off.

We gradually come closer and closer together and she lets me put my arm around her and even kiss her. However, each time my hand wanders off to where she thinks it shouldn't be she gently picks it up and places it back where it came from.

Time flies, and it has started to get dark outside. Akna stands up and straightens out her clothes. "My uncle will be back soon, David. You had better go, but I'll see you off at the plane tomorrow."

Next day, Mum and Dad take me to the airport and Akna is already there, sitting by a long window reading a magazine. My parents are very curious to meet her, and she is equally curious to meet them. About us there is the usual bustle, people dragging big suitcases, waving at each other across the hall, shuffling forward in long lineups. Between my parents and Akna there seems to be an immediate understanding and that makes my heart glad. As I pass through security, I look back at her. I am already wondering when we will be able to see each other again.

30

In early January, I telephone her and she tells me that she has a chance to come to Montreal. "The Inuit government is asking me to go. They want me to travel back with a boy from Postville who has been in hospital with pneumonia. It would be next Tuesday."

"You must come," I tell her. "I'll show you the sights."

I go to the airport and wait for her in the arrivals lounge, my heart literally bursting. When she appears, we stand there for a moment looking at each other. She smiles at me, and I have the extraordinary feeling that her smile is one she could never give to anyone else; it is exclusively mine. "Hello, David," she says softly.

I take her in my arms, and we melt together, oblivious of everything and everybody around us. We are in a world of our own.

We take the bus into Montreal and go to the hostel where she is to stay. She leaves her bag off and we set out on foot together. She is wearing a pale blue parka embroidered with red and yellow patterns that her mother made for her. The hood is trimmed with wolf fur and the cuffs are in rabbit. Wherever we go, arm in arm, the heads turn. She is my Princess-of-the-North.

We go first to Atwater Market. "Who is going to eat all that?" she asks, looking in wonder at the heaps of vegetables and fruit set out beautifully in one of the stands. I am particularly amused at the fish shop, where after examining the halibut, cod and other fish on display, she asks why there is no seal meat. "It's the best of all," she tells the man behind the counter.

Upstairs, we admire the bakery and all the butchers' stalls. "There are so many people," she exclaims. "More here in this little place than in the whole of Goose Bay!"

At the end of the afternoon, Greg and Vreni join us and we go for a pizza together in a nearby restaurant. Vreni and Akna immediately hit it off. At one point there are giggles as Vreni explains that her nickname for Greg is "Gregarious". "I call David 'Mister-too-quickly'," Akna says. Vreni looks at me inquisitively and bursts out laughing.

The four of us remain a long while in the pizzeria, chatting happily and finishing our wine. Akna and I then leave and walk slowly back to the hostel, enveloped in an increasing awareness that something big is happening to us. Outside on the sidewalk, she turns to me. "David. I'm frightened."

"Frightened, Akna? Frightened by what?"

"I don't know. I didn't expect it would come to this, you and me."

She pulls me tightly to her and looks away. "David. I love you," she murmurs into the thickness of my parka.

I am swept by emotion. "Then why are you frightened?"

"We come from such different places. You come from here, this enormous city. I...I come from nowhere, a tiny village lost somewhere up in the north."

"Akna," I try to kiss her, but her face is still buried in my coat. "I love you, too. And there are no good or bad places to come from. Just good or bad people."

Finally, she allows me to kiss her, but then she wrenches herself away from me and disappears inside the hostel.

The next morning, she is busy visiting the boy from Postville and getting him ready for their trip home. That afternoon, I meet her at the hostel and take her around to meet Elka. Neither of us mentions our final conversation of the previous evening. "Will I meet your uncle?" she asks. "The one who brought you up."

"I would prefer not," I answer. "It's so complicated." I explain to her that Leo thinks that he is actually my father.

"That is complicated," she says, "but is it all that important? I mean, whether he is your father or your uncle? Maybe not."

Elka welcomes us with open arms and appears delighted with my choice of girlfriend. She clearly is not about to surrender her role as my surrogate mother, even if the real one has now come to light. We talk for a long while over a cup of tea, Akna taking the opportunity to ask a myriad of questions, many centred on myself. I am a bit distracted and can hear an occasional noise overhead. Leo is there and seems restless.

The time comes for Akna and me to leave. She puts on her magnificent parka and I my rather plebeian one. As we head out the door and back down the street, I sense movement in a window above and glancing back, detect Leo watching us from behind a curtain. I hurry us forward and am only at ease when we have turned the corner.

That evening is to be her last one in Montreal as she and the boy from Postville are booked on a flight the next morning. She asks to see my apartment.

When we arrive, she has a quick look around and throws her parka on a chair. We reach for each other. We exchange words that neither has ever said or heard before. We share feelings that are close to exaltation.

It is as though we can't kiss each other enough, hold each other enough, feel each other enough. The mood is fierce and possessive. We are on fire. We enter another world, a world of song and laughter, of beauty and happiness.

Several weeks later, towards the end of February, Dad announces to me over the phone that he is coming to Montreal and that we are going to have to attempt a reckoning with Leo. "What I have decided, David, rightly or wrongly, is to leave the lawyers out of it at first. It's a gamble, I know. I'm afraid that you'll have to be there just so that Leo believes everything I say, but please let me do all the talking."

I meet him at the airport and we discuss strategy. "When I visited Leo in early January," I tell Dad, "it was pretty bad. He seems to feel that the entire world is conspiring against him, and the fact that I had passed Christmas with you was the supreme insult."

"Did you tell him that your mother was there?"

"No. Of course not."

We go to visit Leo on a Thursday afternoon. He is expecting us, opens the door, gives us a silent look and leads us into the living room.

"Sit down," he says gracelessly.

Dad is calm and looks around the room. "You know,

Leo, I like your house. It must date back quite a while. The nineteen-twenties?"

"About that," says Leo.

"Quiet street too. And well located. Good going."

Leo waits in silence, so Dad continues. "Montreal has changed a lot since we were young. Certainly for the better. How long have you had this house?"

"Going on twenty years." Leo is beginning to show signs of impatience, but Dad just keeps on with the same kinds of remark. Finally, Leo gives a snort. "When are you going to come to the point, Chip? You asked for this meeting, I didn't."

"I think we both need this meeting, Leo. That way, we can avoid a battle that neither of us will win."

Leo is looking for a way forward; you can see it on his face. I watch the two of them, fascinated. Dad edges towards playing his first card. He refers to the fact that it is good that they are trying to do a deal in the absence of their lawyers. "They just cost money. Sometimes, if they don't get along well with each other, they even make things worse. My lawyer's pretty smart and comes from a well-known litigation firm, but I'm not particularly impressed by yours. In any case, I am all in favour of trying to settle matters without them. What do you think?"

"I think my lawyer's fine. He's no rocket scientist, it's true. But he's OK." Both Dad and Leo are aware that Leo's lawyer is far from comfortable in defending Grandad's handwritten will. This is a decided weakness in Leo's position.

Dad continues. "If the handwritten will is set aside, and that with the witnesses is validated, you and I get to divide the estate fifty-fifty. Immediately. What's wrong with that?"

Leo's face goes red. "Where did you find that other

will?" He turns to me. "Was that your doing, David?"

I try to remain calm. "It was in Grandad's papers at the Residence."

"And you found it," Leo continues angrily. I nod. "Why did you give it to your uncle, then? Why didn't you give it to me?"

Dad intervenes. "In the event that we agree to go with the earlier will, the estate could be wrapped up quickly and with it, your administration of Dad's assets while he was still alive. No questions asked." He snaps his fingers. "Like that."

Leo shakes his head angrily. "Screw you, Chip! The hand-written will is in Dad's own hand. It's a scandal that you want to set it aside. You are doing a dishonour to the family going against the wishes of your own father."

Dad begins to lose his cool. "You know the reason perfectly well. Dad wasn't sane of mind when he wrote it. You were almost certainly there when he did it. I bet you dictated every line, every word." Both of them are now beginning to glare at each other.

"Ask him," Leo says, pointing at me. "Ask him if Dad was sane of mind at the time." He turns to me. "Tell him, David. You saw your grandad more often than anyone else. You tell him."

There is a silence. They are both looking at me. "If I was in court and had to tell the judge," I say, "I would have to say that in the last two years of his life, Grandad was never able to think clearly. He was often lost, often confused." You could cut the air with a knife.

Leo explodes. "David! What are you saying? Contradicting your own father." He looks as if he is about to leap from his chair. "And who is that broad you're going about with now? With the fancy parka? She looks like she thinks she's a movie star. Who is she, eh?"

I begin to answer, but Dad calmly interrupts us. "As I was saying, Leo, I would be prepared to accept your earlier administration of Dad's assets. I would ask no questions."

Leo flushes angrily. "There was nothing wrong with my earlier administration. Nothing at all. I have nothing to hide."

"Do you remember how you paid for Miss Steak?" Dad asks. He waits for a reply, but in vain. "Almost forty-six thousand dollars. Three thousand shares of Corinthia Iron and Nickel at fifteen dollars each." Leo looks up. He is stunned that Dad is so well informed. In addition, he is unable to contradict him and so remains silent. "I repeat," Dad says. "It would be so easy for us to be reasonable and make our peace. What have you to lose?"

"Never!" says Leo. "The boat is still there. It hasn't lost any value. It's easy enough for me to show that it belongs to Dad's estate. That way, your accusation doesn't hold water."

Dad smiles maliciously. "We would have to see in whose name the boat is registered and what name appears on the insurance policy. It might also be difficult for you to show that Dad ever went out on the boat." He tries to lower his voice and once more establish room for a compromise. "Tell me. How are you making out with the insurers? Have you received anything yet for the Steak House fire?"

"No," says Leo, "but it should be any time now. I'm on solid grounds there. I was right here in the house when it happened. With David. Nothing to hide there. Isn't that right, David?" Once more, I can feel his eyes on me.

I say nothing. Leo is waiting for me to say something. Dad is trying to look relaxed.

"David," Leo says to me, angrily pointing at Dad. "This bastard here is trying to drive a wedge between us. Can't you see that? He wants to destroy our relationship, all the love that exists between us. Between a father and his son." He is now shouting and waving a fist in the air. "Answer! Was I in the house?"

I say nothing, and Dad comes to my defence. "Leo! You are incapable of thinking of David's interests. You never were good to Valérie. You ripped off your own father. Think of someone other than yourself for a change, you damned fool!"

Leo bounds out of his chair and grabbing a lamp off a nearby table, starts over to where Dad is sitting waving the lamp in the air like a war club. "I'll think of whomsoever I damn well like," he shouts. "You are a feeble do-gooder, Chip. You always were. And you lack staying power; you're a quitter. I'll never quit, so watch out!"

Now Dad and I are also on our feet. I try to get between them. "Stop!" I shout at Leo as he brandishes the lamp. I hold out my arm, and he brushes it aside angrily.

"Whose side are you on anyway?" he roars. "Your father's or your uncle's?"

"You're wrong," I shout back. "You're completely wrong. You aren't my father. You're not my real father at all."

Leo turns to me. "Say that again and I'll kill you!"

"It's true," I repeat. "You aren't my father."

Leo turns from me to Dad and from Dad to me. Dad tries to get between us. "It's true, Leo. Val has confirmed it to us."

Leo flings the lamp at Dad's head, barely missing both me and him. "So, who is the real father? What does that bitch say about that, eh?"

"I am David's father," Dad yells, "and you can like it or lump it!"

With a roar, Leo pushes me aside and rushes at Dad with his head down, tackling him around the waist. The

two of them fall to the ground together amongst the ruins of the lamp. They wrestle there violently. Leo pummels Dad in the face two or three times and Dad begins to bleed above one eye. However, he manages to roll Leo beneath him and taking Leo's head between his hands, bangs it hard on the floor several times. Leo then tries to sit up and Dad butts him fully in the face with the top of his forehead. There is a crunching noise. Leo gives an awful scream of pain; his nose is broken.

Now they are both bleeding profusely, and they writhe together in a vicious tangle in the middle of the living room floor, exchanging blows and gasping for breath. I dance around the periphery, shouting and trying to pull them apart, but it is of no use. After a while the fight begins to lose its most brutal edge as both Leo and Dad are becoming exhausted. In turn, they lie there panting in a heap before they try once more to hit each other.

The end comes unexpectedly when Leo rises slowly from the floor and stumbles towards the kitchen, holding a bloody handkerchief to his nose. He looks at me. "Tell me it's not true, Davie," he says pathetically, pointing at Chip. "He's lying. Isn't he?"

I feel terrible but have no choice. "No," I say. "He is not lying. Mum has confirmed it to us both. Chip is my father, not you."

32

Mid-term break comes along and I go to join Dad in Goose Bay for our long-promised ski-doo trip to Nain. We try to avoid discussing the terrible fight between Dad and Leo, but it is never far from our minds. I have told Akna about the trip, and we plan to see each other when Dad and I pass through Makkovik.

The snow conditions are perfect and we pile all of the things that we will need for the trip in Dad's garage. Dad has borrowed a second machine for me. His is the more powerful, as he will pull a sled behind him with our tent, stove, axe, food, clothes, sundry equipment and several extra tanks of gasoline.

Dad has figured out what route we should take. He has been planning things for a good while, with maps, GPS waypoints and the like. "We have a choice of routes, David. The easy way is the Trans Labrador Trail, which is travelled by a fair number of people and periodically cleared of windfalls and so forth. I think we should take it on our way north. Coming home we can get more inventive if we like. On our first day, we hope to make it to

Makkovik. If not, I know of a cabin partway along where we can spend the night."

In spite of preparations, the fight between Dad and Leo remains constantly in our minds. "I'm worried," Dad says. "What really hit him was to learn that you are not his son."

My friend Andrew drops in on the afternoon before we leave to see how we are getting on. "That's a good route," he confirms. "I have taken it many times."

"How come?" I ask.

"To play hockey. Each winter, I go north with our team by ski-doo and we play against the team in Natuashish."

"Will I find it difficult? I've never done this before."

Andrew laughs. "You'll enjoy it. It's easy. But watch out! My mom says that there are maidens along the way waiting to lure you out onto the ice when the moon is bright. I'll admit," he adds with a laugh, "that I've never seen any."

We plan to leave early the next morning and Dad calls Mum in Baie-Comeau, but there is no reply. Thirty minutes later he tries again, but still there is no reply. "That's funny," he says to me. "I would have expected her to call us to wish us a safe journey, but she hasn't done so."

Then at six in the evening, our phone rings and I pick up the receiver. "*Salut, chéri.* I'm in Forestville. With Armand."

"That's nice," I answer. "Are you there for long?"

"When do you leave?" she wants to know. "When do you start your trip?" There is something unusual about her voice. I sense an urgency in her questions.

"Tomorrow morning, early." I can hear Chip picking up the other phone in the kitchen. "Hello, Dear," he says.

"Chip," she says. "He came. Leo." Her voice begins to sound tight. "I'm alright. I'm fine, and safe here with

Armand."

"Why? What happened Val?" Chip asks anxiously. For my part, I can feel butterflies rising in my stomach.

Mum speaks in a rush. "Leo drove up from Montreal, and without warning came knocking on my door. About two this afternoon. He banged so hard I thought he'd knock it down. Luckily, before I opened it, I called a colleague at school and asked him to come join me in case there was trouble." Her voice starts to shake and she pauses for a moment. "My friend said he would come in twenty minutes, but Leo was making so much noise outside that I let him in."

"He came in like a storm and slammed the door behind him. He even bolted it, to my horror. He then started in about my supposed infidelity. I reminded him that we hadn't been married for twenty years, and that he had been about as unfaithful as a husband could possibly be."

"He asked for you, David. He wanted to know where you were. When I said that you were in Goose Bay, I almost said that you were with your father. Then I realised that I was perhaps saying too much. I simply couldn't remember, so I said that you were there with Chip."

"He said that I had turned you, David, against him. That I had poisoned your mind. That I wanted you all for myself."

"The next thing I knew, Leo had me by the shoulders. He was shaking me, and I tried to fight back. 'Is it true?' he asked. 'Is it true about you and Chip?' I didn't know what he meant, and just shook my head, refusing to answer. I suppose I was crying by then."

"But are you alright, Mum?" I manage to ask.

She continues without answering. "Leo had a strange look on his face. 'Who is David's father?' he wanted to know. 'It's me, isn't it? Answer!' His hands were squeezing my shoulders so hard it hurt." I can hear Chip clearing his throat on the other line.

"I tried to calm him, to gain time," Mum continues. "Anything to stop him from touching me. 'Leo,' I said. 'Please, let's sit down and be calm. If you want me to speak to you, you have to let me remain calm.' He let go of me."

"We sat down. I told him that you, Chip, and I had spent that one night together. I reminded him that during that period he was always away with other women and that he had never wanted to spend any time with me. In short, yes, it was true. It was true that David was not his son."

Chip manages to intervene. "This is terrible, Val. We're going to come down to Baie-Comeau to join you right away."

"No, no. I'm alright now," she says. "Let me finish. He jumped up and swore at me. He hit me several times across the face, calling me a whore, a slut. I pleaded with him to stay quiet, to be reasonable. I was pretty frightened. I was beginning to think that he would kill me."

"He then called you, Chip, by all sorts of names, and said that you would pay for it. He also accused you of poisoning David's mind against him."

"Then he started talking about the estate, of how he had taken care of his father's affairs and found him a place at the Résidence, all of that. I let him talk. I only wanted to gain time."

"Then, there was a curious moment when he started to ask about the amulet. Yes, the amulet of all things. Had I ever come across a little Inuit head carved in stone? With a hole through the back? Had I stolen it from him? Did I know of its whereabouts? Who had it now?"

"I tried to say that I didn't know, and he came over

and hit me in the face again. Hard. 'Answer, or I'll kill you, here and now! Where is it?'. Those were his very words. He asked if I had seen the amulet recently. I said 'yes'. I couldn't see why he was asking, why it was so important to him. I knew that my colleague would be arriving from one moment to the next and so I played for time. I thought I was playing for my life."

"I explained that I had originally found it in his pocket when he came back from a trip up north. He seemed to find that very important and made me repeat it. I then told him I had given it to Grandad, who had taken it with him back to Nain. He asked me who had it now that his father was dead. I tried to avoid saying anything, but he then raised his hand to hit me again and so I told him. I said that you had it, David." We could hear Mum sobbing over the line. "I'm sorry. I shouldn't have, but I just couldn't help it."

We are finally able to interrupt her. "Are you alright though, Val?" Dad asks.

"Oh yes. I'm fine. Luckily my colleague arrived and rang the doorbell several times. I think that by then Leo must have learned all that he wanted to know because he simply put his coat back on and went out the door. I thanked my colleague, locked everything up, and drove to Forestville as fast as I could."

I recognise the voice of Mum's brother Armand saying something to her, and the next moment he is on the line. "Hello, David. Hello, Chip. This is Armand Crevier. Valérie is OK. Don't worry. Just a lot of emotion and a few bruises, but now she's completely safe with me." Chip thanks him and gets his phone number. Mum comes back on the line.

"Armand is right," she says. "I'm fine. Watch out, though. Leo is crazy enough to go on up to Goose Bay and come looking for you."

Dad offers to cancel our trip and to drive down right away to be with her. "Don't even think of it," she says. "In any event Leo's finished with me. It's you I'm worried for."

That night is one of soul-searching. Should we leave on our trip or not? Dad must have spoken to Mum and to Armand about three times. He is very angry with Leo, and Mum doesn't want the two of them to get anywhere close to each other.

The upshot is that we should leave, but that Dad should call her regularly, starting the next day. She assures us that she will be alright and begs us to keep our eye out for Leo. "He once used to keep a pistol. Just make sure you don't take any chances with him. If he shows up, call the police."

I have great difficulty sleeping that night. I feel awful for my mother and furious with Leo. I am ashamed to be in any way associated with him.

33

The next morning, we get up at five. If you can call that getting up. I'm not sure I had any sleep at all. We both have a feeling of foreboding about Leo's whereabouts and intentions. We are uneasy about leaving on the trip, even if it is perhaps the most rational thing to do. "Your mother couldn't be in safer hands," Dad reasons. "Her brother is the chief of police, and in any event, Leo almost certainly doesn't know where she has gone."

"What if he is heading up here?" I ask.

Dad does a quick calculation. "He couldn't arrive here much before this afternoon, even this evening. He doesn't know where I live, at least I don't think so. Lord knows what is on his mind. We can't make it any worse by leaving, so let's go." That settles it, so we rev up our ski-doos and emerge from his garage onto the street, Dad in the lead and I following along behind him. There is plenty of snow on the ground. We are both happy to be leaving Goose Bay behind us.

Our departure is in the dark and it is magic when the sun starts to reveal itself in the eastern sky. There is a red line which grows stronger and stronger beneath the clouds. Gradually the sun appears and tinges in gold the masses of snow weighing down the branches of the black spruce. Where the sun's rays don't penetrate, the shadows are a deep blue.

We make good time and after one hour are past Sheshatshiu, heading for a place called Mulligan.

Usually, we travel at the edge of Lake Melville, on the ice. The going can be rough, and there are moments when we have to proceed cautiously so as not to hit a sharp edge of upturned ice. Dad in particular remains vigilant as he has our sled behind him. Usually I follow in his tracks, but when the travelling is easy, I pull up beside him and we motor along like that, side by side.

By the time we reach Mulligan, it is broad daylight. Mulligan only has a few houses and at most one hundred inhabitants. It is best known, Dad informs me, as the place where a Métis woman named Lydia Campbell lived during the better part of the nineteenth century. Her diaries were published and give a wealth of information on the life that the early inhabitants of Labrador used to lead.

From Mulligan, we turn inland and travel north through a totally uninhabited wilderness. There are no other snowmobile tracks visible, as there has been a recent snowfall. The steep terrain and the deep snow can make the going slow and difficult, particularly for Dad as he is pulling the sled. At more than one point he has to stop, and while I wait at the side of the trail, he goes on ahead with my machine to find a way through and to break trail.

We come to numerous creeks and small rivers, each to be crossed with care as the flow of the water below can weaken the ice.

On the higher ground there are extensive burnlands, places where there has been a forest fire in the recent past.

This can make travelling easier, although you don't want to rub against the branches and get your clothes sooty. Mostly we are on open country, where in the summertime the caribou roam over the mosses. The Labrador tea and crowberry bushes are invisible, buried somewhere beneath us in four feet of snow.

On the very highest spots it can get quite rocky and windswept, and we have to make a careful, circuitous path between patches of ice, scattered boulders and the bare rock.

Periodically, we stop so that Dad can get his bearings. One such moment is lunch. We make a small fire and heat water for our tea. "We're doing alright, David," Dad says, looking up from his map. "I'd say that within an hour, we should reach Separation Lake. How are you managing?"

I am devouring the sandwich which we had made the night before. The night before? It seems as though we left ten days ago. "I'm fine," I say. "A bit stiff in the shoulders, that's all. Is Separation Lake where we spend the night?"

"Yes," says Dad, catching the hint. "As long as we can find the cabin."

We refuel and resume our trip. So far, we have been lucky with the weather. It has been cold and clear. Now, however, a cruel wind picks up, chilling our faces and causing intervals of drifting snow and reduced visibility. I am beginning to look forward to Separation Lake. I wonder how Dad can tell one lake from another. Everything is beginning to look the same to me.

He keeps taking his bearings and eventually I can sense his excitement rising. He peers ahead as if he is expecting to see something. Then comes a moment of triumph. He points at an irregular white expanse below us. "That's it. That's Separation Lake."

We plunge down a series of slopes and finally make

it out onto the ice. Dad checks his GPS a last time and we head off to our left. There, almost invisible under all the snow, is a little cabin. I fervently bless the man or woman who put it there.

There is no sign of recent human presence, but apparently we are welcome to use the cabin. There is even a snow shovel waiting at the door. We stamp our feet to get the circulation back, take turns shovelling, and finally find ourselves inside. All is neat and tidy. There is a stove, a table, two chairs and a bunk bed. The cabin is well provided with firewood and soon we have a fire roaring in the wood stove. It seems to take an eternity to warm the place up, but eventually all is comfortable, our kit is safely indoors, and we can start peeling off our layers of clothing and spreading them about to get dry. Outside the temperature is dropping fast; at a guess it is about minus twenty-five Celsius.

"That was some day, eh?" exults Dad. He is quietly congratulating himself on his skills of navigation. He should be good, I think. He had lots of practice in Hudson Bay. "You did very well for a first time. Did you enjoy it?" He chats on like that, but I know that underneath it all he is really worried about Mum and about whether we have made the right decision.

So I play the game and answer that of course I enjoyed my day. In fact, I am so exhausted that I am beginning to wonder if I'll be able to make it all the way up to Nain and back. Dad is busy organising our supper, and I put out our sleeping bags for the night, leaving them partly open so they can warm up. I take the upper bunk and leave the lower bunk for Dad.

When later on we are lying there in the warmth of our beds I ask Dad what he thinks Leo will do.

"Good question. My guess is that he will have driven

on up to Goose Bay. That means about twelve hours on the road. He could be arriving there any time now."

"Looking for us?"

"Yes. Looking for us."

"So, what do we do?"

"Get a good night's sleep. He certainly won't find us out here on Separation Lake!"

34

When I wake up, the cabin is still fairly warm as Dad has kept the fire going all night. There is a delicious smell of softwood smoke in the air and yes, the smell of bacon. We have a big breakfast, but a rapid one. Dad is anxious for us to get started again. My boots were off in a corner, and when I go to put them on, they are so cold they feel like they are made of cast iron.

Outside as we load up, the sun is just breaking above the hills behind the lake. We're on our way to Makkovik!

We could go on to Postville, further up the coast, but I have told Dad that there is a good hotel in Makkovik and that I have someone there that I would like to see. He grins. "Like Akna?" I don't deny it. So we are taking the trail to Makkovik.

Again, there are easy bits such as the frozen lakes and streams, and tougher bits, particularly climbing up steep hillsides through forests of black spruce. The trail is not in the best of conditions and several times, Dad has to take my ski-doo ahead to break trail.

In mid-afternoon, we arrive triumphant in Makkovik

and pull up in front of the Adlavik Hotel. As soon as he is inside, Dad calls Mum. She is still at her brother's in Forestville, safe and sound. We chat a bit and tell her what we plan for the next day. She says that she has one bad bruise under her left eye, but that's all, and Leo seems to have disappeared. I then call Akna. She sounds anxious to speak to me and says that she will come over to the hotel in twenty minutes.

We meet downstairs for a coffee. I have a little present for her, a jar of honey from Greg's father's farm on Covey Hill. She thanks me, turning it over in her slender hands. "It's such a beautiful colour," she murmurs. "Thank you, David."

She is looking more lovely than ever, but I can tell that something is bothering her. We sit at the window, facing each other and exchanging our news. Dad joins us briefly so as to greet her and then goes back upstairs for a nap. I explain to her that early next morning, we leave and travel over the sea ice to Nain.

A silence comes between us. She looks at me. "My grandfather says he would like to see you again. Could you come to see him?"

"Of course," I answer.

"Do you have the amulet with you? You know, the one you showed us in November?"

"Yes. It's upstairs."

"Could you bring it?"

I go to fetch it, and when I get back downstairs, find her outside starting up her ski-doo. I get on behind, we leave the hotel and we go down to the road running along the edge of the water. It is nice to be a passenger for a change! When we reach her house, we dismount and go inside.

In the hallway, I pause to admire an old photograph.

"Is that you, Akna? The clothing looks different; also the hair."

"No, that is my aunt Sadie when she was my age. We look alike, don't we?" She leads me into the room where Ittuq is seated, his shoulders wrapped in a heavy grey blanket.

He is wearing dark glasses and looks frail. All the same, he greets me warmly.

I tell him of the snowmobile trip that Dad and I are making. There is a pause and he says something to Akna. She turns to me. "He says he would like to hold the amulet again."

I pull it out of my pocket and place it in the old man's hands. For the longest of times, we hold our breath as he turns it over, first in one direction and then in the other. He starts to talk again, with Akna as his interpreter.

"This is it. This is the one I gave to Sadie. I can feel it - it is talking to me." He pauses. "The amulet is good, David. It is good that you should have it and that you are here now. Keep it with you at all times and be careful." I can't for the life of me understand why he is telling me all this, but I ask no questions and he appears to have said all that he wishes to say.

Akna rises and offers to take me back to the hotel. "David," she says when we arrive. "There is something more that you should know. My mother told it to me only yesterday. Before Sadie drowned, she had been spending time with a man from Goose Bay, someone who was unknown to the family and whom no-one ever saw afterwards. My mother says that when Sadie died, she was pregnant."

I am appalled. "Akna," I say uncertainly. "If as Ittuq says, my amulet is the same as the one that your aunt Sadie once wore, then the man who used to see her and who made her pregnant was almost certainly my uncle Leo. He was living here in Labrador at the time. One day, he returned to Goose Bay from a trip up here and my mother found the amulet in his pocket. She kept it hidden and then gave it to my grandad. That's how I now have it."

A strange look comes across Akna's face. "He must have taken it from Sadie," she murmurs.

"Does anyone know how she drowned?" I ask.

"Not really. Ittuq found her body in Ugjoktok Bay, that was all. But he says that if it had been an accident, she would have still had the amulet on her. He thinks that there must have been a struggle during which the amulet came off or was torn off." Akna stands there looking at me.

I am devastated. That was almost certainly Leo! He got her pregnant. Then perhaps in order to be rid of an embarrassing problem, he murdered her. Is that what happened? Leo? The man who brought me up? How can I walk down a street in Makkovik, or in any other Labrador town with my head held high? Akna and I look speechlessly at each other.

"David," she says hesitantly. "Don't feel badly. It's not your fault." Her eyes are misting and she bites her upper lip. "Maybe we should stop seeing each other. You will surely find someone else. You are so gentle, so kind. Any girl would be happy to go with you. I am not so special." Now she is crying, and she wipes her eyes with her sleeve. "In any event, I always intended to marry an Inuk. I always wished my children to be Inuit. I guess that's what it will be." She turns away quickly and gets on her ski-doo. "Goodbye, David," she waves, and is gone.

35

The light comes on in our room. Dad is shaking my shoulder. I feel rotten, but stumble out of bed. He shoves a cup of coffee into my hands and it burns my throat. I dress. Without exchanging a word, we cart our things downstairs, go out into the silent cold, load up our machines, and coast as quietly as we can down the hill to the water's edge.

The memory of my parting with Akna comes back to me as we descend onto the ice of the inlet. I wonder how she feels, and whether she and I will manage to see each other again. I try to put it out of my mind so I can concentrate on following Dad, but then the memory of our magical night together in Montreal comes flooding back to me and I can barely contain my tears.

Then I think of my mother, and of what Leo did to her. I imagine him hitting her. I think of her pain, her terror. I feel guilty that she should have gone through all that on my account, just because Leo wanted to track me down, me and the amulet.

Dad and I had discussed this as we lay in our beds the previous evening. "I now know why Leo wants to get his hands on the amulet, David," he had said to me. "It is the one thing that can connect him with Sadie's death."

Is that so, and is Leo a murderer? Is he now gunning for Chip and for me? Can a simple Inuit carving carry all that significance? Why did Ittuq say that it was good that I was in Makkovik, and good that I should have the amulet with me? Why did he say that I should be careful? What does he know that I don't know?

I try to forget about all this and to concentrate on driving along behind Dad, but I have the terrible conviction that I don't know where I am going and I don't know what is about to happen. My future and even my life are suspended in the hands of fate.

Makkovik is now well behind us. The early morning sun is somewhere out there on our right hand, beyond a white haze. The ice is rough and the going is difficult. Dad picks his way ahead avoiding the worst patches and I tag along behind. He is worried about the hitch attaching the sled to his snowmobile. It is taking a beating with all the rough ice that we have been crossing. He is afraid that it will break. If he were to hit some upturned ice and stop suddenly, the hitch could snap and the sled could bounce up and hit him from behind.

I am beginning to find driving a ski-doo tremendously monotonous. My mind tends to drift off, lulled by the motion and by the constant sound of the engine seeping through my helmet. *Leo and Sadie, Sadie and Leo.* I just can't get them out of my mind as I bump along over the ice, stubbornly following Dad's tracks and pressing on in order to keep up with him. I try to imagine where Leo is and what may be going on in his mind, and have difficulty controlling a mounting feeling of apprehension. "Are we heading for disaster?" I ask myself. "What's going to happen?" Mechanically, I reach a hand down and tap my pocket - the amulet is there, reassuringly pressing against my leg. Once more, I think of what Ittuq said the day before.

As the day wears on, the visibility ahead and to seaward dissolves increasingly into a white haze and Dad stops, looking anxious. "We've passed Kaipokok Bay," he tells me, looking at his map and swearing softly to himself, "and I would say that this land coming up on our right is Kikkertavak Island. If so, we're off course, and worse still, we're behind schedule. I think we should head further inland. At least in that direction, we'll be able to see where we're going."

The more towards the mainland we go, the smoother the ice becomes. In addition, the haze dissipates and we are able to travel a bit faster. At a certain point, we even stop for a breather and a quick bite. Once more, Dad pulls out his map.

"David. I'm sorry, but today is turning out to be more difficult than I had expected. I also don't like the colour of the sky. It looks like snow to me. We need to take a decision. Either we stay out here in the open, or we go even closer to shore, where we can find shelter if we need to. In fact, there's no choice. If we stay out here and don't make it all the way to Hopedale, we'll have no firewood, no fire to warm us up, and we'll freeze to death."

"Where are we exactly, Dad? What are the distances?"

"Hard to tell. In two hours, we could get back to Postville. In two or three hours, we might make it to Hopedale. Just."

"And to shore?"

"Oh! Half an hour, I suppose. Perhaps forty-five minutes. If that's what we choose to do, we can look for shelter, find ourselves a nice stand of spruce somewhere, and put up the tent."

"Where exactly are we now?" I ask, looking over his shoulder at the map.

"There," he points with his finger. "We are entering Ugjoktok Bay."

Ugjoktok Bay.

I feel a sense of foreboding. Dad looks at me and I at him. He is also shaken by the association. We think of Grandad's words when he gave me the amulet: *Where the seals gather.*

We think of Ugjoktok Bay, the place where Sadie drowned.

It seems surreal that we should be arriving at this place and in these circumstances. I try to put my thoughts behind me, to forget about Sadie and about Leo.

"Sorry," I say, "but I'm dead. I can't keep this up for another three hours. I just can't. Let's stop somewhere, and can we please go a bit slower? It's hard to keep up with you."

Dad folds up his map and off we go, turning inland almost at right angles from our previous course. The afternoon is slipping by and it feels like snow.

After twenty minutes or so, Dad stops and announces to me that we had better fill up our tanks with gas, which we do. "The last thing we want is to run low at the wrong time." I watch him as he gets back on his ski-doo. I can see that he has something on his mind. He hesitates. "David. Do you hear something?"

I listen and can hear nothing. Dad shakes his head and off we go. He is in the lead. After another twenty minutes he stops and signals to me to turn off my engine. This time I can hear it. Far behind us, the sound of another ski-doo. Dad waves his hand at me and we take a new direction towards our right. Ten minutes later, we stop and listen again. The noise is still there, following us with each change of direction. We turn to our left and head into the gathering twilight. The wind is now rising in the east and a heavy wet snow is starting to fall.

I am beginning to feel overcome with exhaustion. My forearms are aching and I have difficulty holding the ski-doo steady. I also find my mind wandering, so that from time to time I have to sit up straight and stare ahead just to keep my eyes open.

We switch on our headlights, and it isn't always easy to see because of the big snowflakes that are now falling in profusion and sticking to the visors of our helmets. They fill the tracks behind us as soon as they are made. They smother the landscape, making everything white, everything the same. It almost makes you dizzy, the way it confuses up with down.

One final time, we stop and turn off our engines. By now, we can barely discern a line of trees close on our left. We listen, and the ski-doo is still following us. Dad dismounts and comes over to me. "David. Someone is deliberately following us and he's getting closer and closer. It may be because he is lost. But it may also be because he wants to catch up with us. It could be Leo. He's that crazy. I don't like it at all. Whoever it is, let's try to shake him off."

I agree and wonder what an encounter out here with Leo might lead to. Out here in Ugjoktok Bay. I am afraid for Dad. In fact, I am afraid for both of us.

Dad looks behind us once more. "Without my sled we can go a lot faster." He quickly unhitches the sled from behind his snowmobile, jumps on his machine and waves at me to follow him. He sets off in a new direction at top speed.

I bend over the handlebars of my machine and drive like I haven't driven before, trying desperately to stay in his tracks and to keep up with him. Gigantic snowflakes are whirling through the air like autumn leaves and in the glare of our headlights their effect is blinding. Above our heads the sky is a dull grey emptiness. Dad has to slow down from time to time so that I can keep up. Our progress is more rapid without the sled.

We see an opening in the bank of trees to our left. It must be a creek. Dad heads in its direction and I follow in his tracks. It becomes steep and we are forced to turn this way and that in order to make it up the slope. Still, we succeed. We quickly look back and can just see the headlight of a ski-doo flashing up and down in the darkness, stubbornly following in our tracks. Off we go again!

We are now on flat ground somewhat above and to the south of the estuary of the Ugjoktok River. It is the sort of terrain that in summertime is bog, covered with Labrador tea and other small shrubs. I am following in Dad's tracks at a fair clip. Suddenly, I hear a sound that literally makes the hair stand up on the nape of my neck. It is the sound of a bullet whining past me from behind, followed almost at once by a sharp *CRAAAK*, also coming from behind. I lean as low as I can over my machine as a second shot passes over my head.

36

Dad has stopped abruptly. His taillights warn me. I come to a halt just behind him, so weak that I almost fall off my machine. A ski-doo has arrived from our right at great speed. It stops in front of us and the driver stands up in the machine and urgently signals to us.

I immediately recognise that slim profile, the long black hair sticking out from beneath the helmet. It is Akna! Nothing could do more to jolt me out of my torpor, to give me new heart. She points urgently to a group of trees on our left, signalling to us that we should go in amongst them with our machines.

Dad understands what is meant, and turning his machine hard left, he disappears into the little wood. I do likewise, and watch Akna out of the corner of my eye as she rapidly wheels her snowmobile around in a tight circle and brings it about so that it is placed in our former tracks.

Dad and I turn our machines and lights off and wait. The headlight of the other ski-doo appears in the gloom to our right, and Akna takes off, at first tentatively, but once she sees that the other machine is following her, at breakneck speed, careening left and right between the stunted trees and deadfalls and setting a course that only a madman could follow. As the other machine passes by in front of where we are hidden, we can recognise Leo, rigidly hunched over and staring stubbornly ahead. I am afraid for Akna's safety. She has appeared out of nowhere in order to help us shake off Leo, but what if something happens to her?

The noise of their two engines gradually disappears and for a while we are left in the darkness guessing where they have gone. My only thought is to find them, to stop Leo from doing anything to Akna. However, in the obscurity of that snowstorm, it is difficult to know what to do. Dad chooses to take us prudently forward and stops from time to time in order to listen. At one point, he consults his map in the glare of my headlight.

Now he raises his head and points to his ear. He can hear them again.

We have come to the top of a steep, wooded bank that seems to descend into a black void. I can guess that down below, there is a frozen stream, almost certainly a tributary of the Ugjoktok. We can hear the sound of an engine approaching somewhere on our left. It seems to be travelling on the frozen stream below. There is no way we can take our ski-doos down that steep bank. It is choked with trees and deadfalls. We stop our engines and look down.

A single light has appeared below us and on our left, its beam losing itself in the snow that is falling thick and fast ahead of it. It approaches slowly and pauses immediately opposite us. It then turns hard to its left, and in the instant before the light is extinguished, we can see that the snowmobile has hidden itself behind a big deadfall that crosses most of the stream from the far side.

That must be Akna. We wait for what seems an eternity.

A second light is now approaching. It is presumably Leo. Dad waves to me urgently. We get off our machines and struggle through the snow to the top of the bank. The snow is very deep and it is desperate work going through it. However, we know that something is going to happen down there, that Akna will be face to face with Leo, and that we must help as best we can. I lose sight of Dad in all that snow as I start stumbling and rolling down the bank. I hit a tree hard, my shoulder screams and the breath is knocked out of me. I get stuck under a deadfall and have to struggle uphill to extract myself. I am about halfway down the bank and look out to see what is happening below. The second machine is approaching steadily, approaching the deadfall where Akna is hidden.

A body smashes into me from above. It is Dad. We are in such a tangle in the deep snow that I can hardly tell which way is up. We separate ourselves and continue down the slope, each choosing his own way.

I hear the sound of Leo's ski-doo as it comes up. He slows down beside the deadfall and his taillights turn bright red. I fall over some low branches and for a moment lose sight of everything. There is a tangle of alders at the bottom of the bank and I pull on them desperately, but they just yield when I pull and they give me no support. I try to roll over them, to burrow through them, anything to get out there onto the bank of the stream. At last, I am through.

I stagger to my feet. The storm has stopped as if by magic. I look up and see the black sky studded by a million stars. There is a moon, close to being full. In the distance, a lone wolf can be heard. It has suddenly become much colder and I am shivering.

Leo's machine is thirty feet in front of me, stopped

beside the deadfall with its engine turning over. He is astride the seat, still wearing his helmet, but with the strap hanging loose and the visor thrown up. His back is turned towards me. Standing not far beyond him beside her own machine is Akna, dressed in a dark coverall. She is holding her helmet in one hand, and I can see her face, pale and beautiful in the moonlight. Her other hand rests on the seat of her machine. She is confronting him and they are motionless.

Before I can say or do anything, Leo turns away from her violently and revs up his engine. It bucks and jumps ahead across the ice. Beyond a short expanse of white, all is black. This is where Akna has led him!

Leo's machine lurches ahead and then stops with a roar. Its headlights search crazily in the sky. I can see the ski-doo tilt to one side. Its front seems to swing around towards me and then the rear end disappears down through the ice. The next thing I know, the engine has stopped and the lights go out. Close beyond, I can now see open water, where the river is flowing black with golden ripples in the gleam of the moon. I can hear the river in the new silence which envelopes us. There is a constant rushing noise.

Leo has now climbed precariously onto the hood of his machine. Somehow he has lost his helmet. For a moment I have a glimpse of his face, and although I can hear nothing, his mouth is open and he appears to be shouting.

Dad has now joined me and we watch in horror as Leo clumsily tries to cross from the hood of his machine onto the ice beside it. He lunges across, but the ice breaks under his weight and he falls sideways into the water. His arms wave, first the one then the other. He is trying to regain his balance, to stay out of the deep coldness of

the water even as it slowly seeps into his boots and fills up the legs of his snowmobile suit. His is a black profile struggling against a black and white background. It is terrible to see.

Dad is looking around, trying to see if there is any way he can get out there to help his brother. I start forward and after several steps can feel the ice beginning to yield under me. Dad is at my side and, seizing me by the arm, pulls me back to safety. "Don't try, David," he shouts. "The ice won't hold you."

Leo's clothes will be getting wet. They will weigh him down. When he struggles onto another bit of ice, it too will break off. He will be paralysed by the cold water and will get weaker as his efforts fail. But the current of the river will not become weaker. It will pull at him, drag him, suck him down. He will take one last look upwards and see the stars that fill the huge black sky above. He will reach out one arm in a futile gesture, staring towards us, staring also at the girl standing next to her snowmobile, and his mouth will open as if to cry out, but no sound will emerge. His body will slip gradually under the ice, to be claimed by the freezing waters of the Ugjoktok.

I am numb, and stand there in horror, watching as he perishes. I turn towards Akna, but she too has vanished from sight. Then I do see her, collapsed in the snow nearby. I kneel at her side. Blood is coming slowly out of a small hole in her ski jacket at the back of the shoulder. Panic sweeps over me and I call Dad urgently.

37

My thoughts are in turmoil as I walk down the hallway of the hospital in Goose Bay. The past several days have been unlike anything I have ever experienced in my life. There has been the constant worry for Akna. Will she pull through? Will she suffer any long-term effects?

She had surgery yesterday and it seems that they were able to remove the bullet and all of the bone fragments. They say that her condition is stable, that all things considered she is doing pretty well. Now she is allowed to receive visitors. Her mother was there with her just before me.

She smiles when I enter the room and reaches out her hand, which I gently squeeze. It then disappears again beneath the covers. I ask her how she feels. The reply is short, but reassuring.

"Finc, David. Just sleepy. Thanks for coming."

"Thank you for saving my life!"

She gives me a little smile, her special smile. "Thank Ittuq. He sent me."

"How did he know?"

"We heard a man had arrived on the plane, spoken to someone at the hotel, stolen a ski-doo. I told Ittuq."

"And he sent you to tell me?"

"Yes."

"You were very brave doing what you did. Weren't you afraid?"

"A little. Specially at the end."

"I saw him look at you. Perhaps you made him think of Sadie."

"Perhaps."

The scene comes back to me: Leo staring at her, looking back to the front, driving his snowmobile straight ahead. I suddenly know that his act was deliberate.

"I'm sorry he died, but perhaps it had to happen. It's just funny it was me," she says. "What happened afterwards?"

"Dad and I got you back to Hopedale and you were taken down here right away by air ambulance. I stayed up there with Dad at the hotel, but had a fever. Now I'm better. We came down to Goose Bay yesterday. My mother is here with us. We're all recovering from the shock."

"I'm feeling better too."

"They say you're doing really well. Does it hurt?"

"Not much." She smiles.

"Can I continue to come to see you?" I ask.

She reaches out her hand and gives mine another quick squeeze. "Of course."

"I'm very sorry, Akna," I tell her. "About my uncle Leo and Sadie, I mean. You can't imagine how ashamed I feel."

"Ittuq says it's not your fault. He told my mother." She stirs under the covers. "My foot has gone to sleep. Ouch. The right one. Can you rub it for me?"

I rub it for a while through the blanket. "That's better. Thanks. Ittuq says that the amulet made all this happen.

You, me, your uncle's death. He says Sadie is now at peace."

"The amulet?"

"Yes, the amulet. He says that is why your grandad gave it to you."

A nurse appears and asks if everything is alright. Akna nods and the nurse leaves again after giving me a look that says that she thinks it is time for me to go. "Will you come back tomorrow, David?" Akna asks.

"Of course," is my answer.

"Good." She turns her head fully towards me. "Ittuq says it is now alright for us to go with each other. He says the amulet has bound us together."

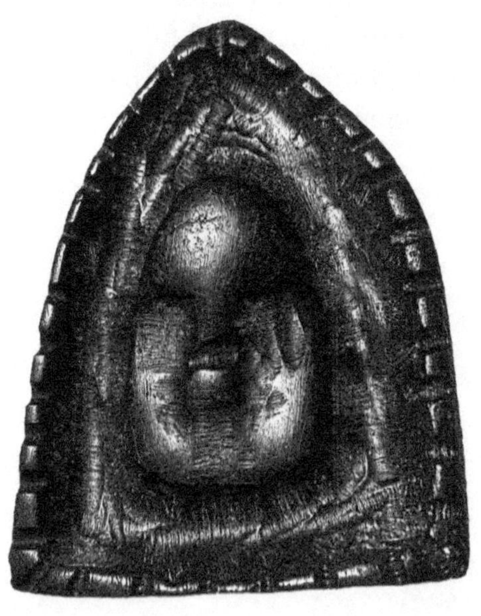

I would like to thank Stewart Learning of Cartwright and Paradise River for the wonderful times we have enjoyed canoeing together in Central Labrador.

I would also like to thank Meg Graham for her helpful comments on an early draft of this book.

Finally, my thanks go to Paul Abraham for the cover and illustrations, and to Aaxel Author Services for their editorial and technical support.